"You seem quite at home near the water, Miss Leslie, yet I believe you come from the Midlands, do you not?"

"I do. But my mother is Scottish, and my brothers and I spent our summers on Loch Lomond. I swim like a fish."

"How intriguing." His gaze roamed the length of her body as if he were gauging her buoyancy. "What sort of fish?"

"Does it matter?"

"Certainly. Fish are quite different, you know. There are those which swim near the surface, stopping now and then to snatch a dragonfly. Others stay near the bottom, flitting over the sand and feeding off scraps other creatures leave behind, drab in color and usually quite ugly. Then there are fish who swim near the middle, neither too cold nor too warm, too dark nor too light. Those fish, of course, are the most vibrant and colorful." He stopped and looked her over once again. "Yes, I believe you'd be that sort of fish. Beautiful, swift, and clever, gracefully dancing in the rays of the sun filtering through the water."

Judith's mouth dropped open. Never had anyone called her beautiful, let alone graceful.

"I've rendered you speechless. Is that a first?"

Judith snapped her mouth shut. "Yes, I rather think it is. What a lovely thing to say. I'm sure no one has ever used any of those words to describe me, let alone all of them in a single sentence."

He reached out and stroked her cheek. "They are all true."

# Treasure Her Heart

by

Marin McGinnis

This is a work of fiction. Names, characters, places, and incidents are either the product of the author's imagination or are used fictitiously, and any resemblance to actual persons living or dead, business establishments, events, or locales, is entirely coincidental.

**Treasure Her Heart**

COPYRIGHT © 2018 by Marin Ritter

All rights reserved. No part of this book may be used or reproduced in any manner whatsoever without written permission of the author or The Wild Rose Press, Inc. except in the case of brief quotations embodied in critical articles or reviews.
Contact Information: info@thewildrosepress.com

Cover Art by *Rae Monet, Inc.*

The Wild Rose Press, Inc.
PO Box 708
Adams Basin, NY 14410-0708
Visit us at www.thewildrosepress.com

Publishing History
First Tea Rose Edition, 2018
Print ISBN 978-1-5092-2183-7
Digital ISBN 978-1-5092-2184-4

Published in the United States of America

# Dedication

To Gina.

Chapter 1

*London, 1832*

The occasion of one's debut was an odd mixture of excitement, fear, boredom, and an overwhelming desire to toss one's breakfast. But The Honorable Judith Leslie had never been one to waste food, so her breakfast remained where it ought, and she curtsied to King William and his queen without mishap.

She executed an uncharacteristically graceful turn and was led out of the presence of the monarchs. At the age of nineteen, she was older than all of this year's debs, and at least a head taller, a fact most of them were all too happy to mention.

"Does the air up there smell different, I wonder?" one of them, Lady Cassandra, said to another as Judith passed. The eldest daughter of the Duke of Bothwell, Cassandra was pert, pretty, and petite with an English roses and cream complexion and had been bullying Judith at every opportunity.

Judith was—as her mother liked to say with a surprising lack of irony—statuesque, with a ruddy complexion and auburn hair that tended to escape from its pins. Being half Scottish, she often thought she was better suited to a Highland sheep farm than a London ballroom.

Judith's mother, Lady Grangemore, caught up to

her and gave Lady Cassandra a withering glare that only made the snooty girls snicker.

"Ignore them," she said to Judith.

Judith had been tempted to elbow Cassandra in the head but was, of course, far too well-mannered to do it. "I always do," she lied.

"You were marvelous in there, my dear. The other girls appeared mere sparrows in comparison to your swan-like beauty."

Her mother spent far too much time reading novels. "Thank you, Mama, but I'd hardly call myself swan-like."

"Nonsense. Of course you are." Lady Grangemore sniffed in dismissal of her daughter's protest and surveyed the buffet table, heavy with food. "What on earth is that creation, do you think? It seems to be moving." She pointed to an ice sculpture on the table—a giant tree, graced with tiny birds in such striking detail they appeared to be flying.

"The palace spares no expense for the start of the Season, I suppose. Although I can't imagine how they'll keep it from melting all over the sweetmeats. It's unseasonably warm today, don't you agree, Mama?"

"Hmph," her mother said, clearly uninterested in the weather. "Shall we go, my dear? We do have your own ball preparations to finish. Such a coup to be able to schedule it for today. Lady Bothwell practically spat as I walked by her this morning." Lady Grangemore didn't rub her hands together in maniacal glee, but her fingers twitched with anticipation.

Judith didn't know how her mother, a viscountess from Derbyshire, had managed to upstage the Duchess of Bothwell in scheduling the very first ball of the season, but she did know her mother had been planning the debutante ball for her only daughter since the day she was born. A woman so motivated is not to be underestimated.

She listened to her mother's prattle with half an ear as their carriage rumbled away from the palace toward their townhouse in Mayfair. Judith missed their home in Derbyshire, with her horses, her dogs, a society of people she'd known her entire life. Since arriving in London two months before, she'd been poked and prodded within an inch of her life as seamstresses measured and fitted God only knew how many new dresses and ensembles. As Judith didn't have many friends in London, she spent a lot of time alone, reading, playing the piano, or dragging her maid on long walks through Hyde Park. The London cook wasn't amenable to having her help in the kitchen, unlike the cook at home, so she didn't even have baking to divert her.

She was bored out of her head.

"Judith," Lady Grangemore said, gently swatting Judith with her reticule. "You haven't heard a word I said, have you?"

"Sorry, Mama." Judith smiled, tried to muster more enthusiasm, for her mother's sake.

"Never mind. I am sure you must be exhausted. I know I didn't sleep a wink before my presentation to King George. Why don't you take a little rest before the ball?"

Judith, who'd slept quite soundly, nodded gratefully and disappeared to her bedroom once they arrived home. There was a book she wanted to finish.

\*\*\*\*

Peter Tenwick, Lord Caxton, stood at attention before his father's giant mahogany desk and braced himself. Ordinarily a pleasant, non-confrontational sort of man, the Earl of Longley was in a decidedly different temper today. He'd just received a report of Peter's behavior last evening; not from Peter himself, of course, but from one of the earl's cronies who delighted in reporting the misdeeds of the younger members of the peerage to their parents. The earl was, to put it mildly, rather put out.

"For God's sake, Peter! Caught swimming, nude, in Hyde Park? You're nearly thirty!"

"I fail to see what my age has to do with this," Peter said.

"It has everything to do with this. You are my son and heir. You still behave like a fool a decade younger, and you haven't so much as looked for a suitable mate."

"Mate? You make me sound like one of your hounds."

Red in the face, nearly apoplectic, the earl took a deep breath. He rubbed a hand over his thinning light hair, his shoulders sinking a bit in resignation. "You know very well what I mean, boy. I am too old for this. I should have had at least four grandchildren to toddle on my knee by now. You need to find a suitable debutante, marry her, and conceive an heir."

Peter helped himself to a tot of brandy from the sideboard. "I have never met a single deb I could pass the time of day with, Father, let alone...anything else."

His father's brow pinched in a scowl, his face paled to a pinkish hue. He waved a hand, exasperated. "You don't have to *talk* to her, Peter. Your mother, God rest her soul, and I barely spoke, and we had four children."

Peter rolled his eyes. Lord and Lady Longley had been very ill suited in temperament, but his mother had assuredly been a good breeder. Unfortunately, three of the four had been girls.

His father wasn't finished. "Today, Peter, or I'll cut you off. Don't think I won't." Given the determined set of his father's jaw, he was quite serious indeed. A niggle of worry lodged in Peter's belly.

Fine. He would start looking, but his father's ultimatum didn't require that he find one. He had no interest in marrying anyone; he'd seen too many of his friends fall prey to shrewish fortune hunters, and his own parents had been so miserable together he saw no need to follow suit.

And he had just the thing to ensure no one would take him seriously.

## Chapter 2

Judith was exhausted.

Her feet throbbed, her cheeks ached from maintaining a perpetual smile, and her eyes stung from the smoke in the air generated by thousands of candles and gentlemen's cigars. She'd danced every dance, and her head was swimming with the names of her partners. Thank goodness for her dance card, since she'd be required to list them all for her mother in order of preference.

Not that her mother hadn't been paying very close attention anyway. She'd probably memorized the rank and income of each of them.

Judith spotted an empty chair along the wall and made a beeline for it, hoping to soothe the feet that had just been trodden upon by Lord Something-or-Other of the Yorkshire Something-or-Others. It was a delicate balance, moving purposefully through the crowd without inadvertently cutting Lady Whosit, elbowing the Dowager Countess Whatsit, or attracting the unwelcome attentions of a pimple-faced lordling. She was nearly to her goal when there was a commotion at the entrance to the ballroom. Judith glanced at her mother's grandfather clock. It was four o'clock in the morning—not at all late to *be* at a ball, but quite unfashionably late to be arriving at one.

A man stood in the doorway. Tall and rugged, he

was, in a word, astonishing. Fashionably mussed as if he'd just risen from bed, his dark blond hair hung over one eye, and he wore a self-satisfied smile suggesting he hadn't been alone there. But it was his waistcoat which drew everyone's attention.

Having abandoned his post at the ballroom door due to the lateness of the hour, the butler sped to the newcomer's side. After a whispered conversation, he turned to the assembly.

"Viscount Caxton," he said in a tone conveying both surprise and disapproval.

Lord Caxton wended his way through the ballroom, nodding to many of the guests. He plucked a glass of champagne off a passing tray and stood near the mantel, his hooded gaze observing those who were observing him. Judith vaguely noticed her feet—somehow no longer sore—move of their own accord until she was standing just in front of him. She blinked, as much to clear her suddenly foggy brain as to relieve her eyes of the sight of his rather mesmerizing coat. She didn't think she'd ever seen so many colors and fabrics in one place, not even at her *modiste*'s. He winked at her, his eyes twinkling with mischief.

He took her hand and bowed over it with a flourish, his hair curling around his bright purple collar. He kissed her hand, straightened, and winked again.

His touch sent tingles screaming up her arm. Judith was so startled she burst out the first thing that came into her head. "Wherever did you find that atrocious coat?"

The crowd surrounding him began to laugh, the ladies tittering behind their fans. Heat flooded Judith's cheeks, but she was rescued from further embarrassment by her mother, who appeared at her side visibly quivering with indignation.

"My lord. Have you been introduced to my daughter?"

"I have not, but I should very much like to be, if this vision before me is she."

Lady Grangemore cocked her head but did not immediately introduce Judith, a notable social gaffe most uncharacteristic of her. Finally, she said, "Lord Caxton, may I introduce my daughter, The Honorable Judith Leslie."

Judith observed this exchange with wide eyes before her mother elbowed her hard in the ribs. Resisting a childish urge to poke right back, Judith instead curtsied to Lord Caxton. "I am pleased to make your acquaintance, my lord."

"And I yours." He bowed again, but Judith kept her hand safely at her side this time.

"I don't believe I received your acceptance of our invitation, Lord Caxton." Lady Grangemore straightened to her full height, regarding Caxton with a rather icy stare.

"Please forgive me, my lady. I did not believe I would be able to attend due to another engagement, but there was an unexpected change in my plans." Lord Caxton's smile was engaging, designed to charm even the most hostile mama. Unfortunately, it didn't seem to be doing much for Judith's.

"How nice for us," she said, in a tone suggesting quite the opposite. "Come along, Judith. There is someone else whom you must meet." An obvious lie, since she'd spent an hour in the receiving line meeting every single attendee. Her mother grabbed her arm in a fierce grip and tugged her away from Lord Caxton. She glimpsed over her shoulder, only to have him wink at her again.

She nearly tripped as her mother all but dragged her through the ballroom. "Mama, stop. What on earth is the matter with you?"

"You should have nothing to do with that man. He's a rake of the worst sort." Her mother wrestled Judith into a corner behind a potted plant and finally released her.

"Why did you invite him, then?" she asked, rubbing her arm.

"Because it would have been rude not to do so, but I dinna for a moment think he'd come. He hasna attended a ball in years."

Lady Grangemore's native Scottish brogue only slipped into her speech when she was highly flustered or upset. Judith scrunched her face to study her mother, wondering what would cause such a reaction to one young man. Noticing her mother's flushed cheeks, she decided it was best to leave the subject for the moment. "And it wasn't rude to drag me away, leaving him standing there on his own?"

Her mother took a deep breath, and the redness in her cheeks faded. She waved her hand in dismissal. "He obviously cares little for social mores. Look at that ridiculous waistcoat he's wearing," she said in a harsh whisper. "It must have a dozen different colors."

Judith peered around the plant, only to find him staring at her, an impish grin plastered upon his outrageously handsome face. "Ouch!" Her mother had grabbed her arm once more, pulling her back.

Studying Judith, she said, "You seem tired, darling.

Perhaps it's time for you to retire. It's been such a long day."

Curiosity overcame fatigue. "I'm not in the least tired, Mama. I believe there is one more dance, correct? And I just happen to have it open." In an act of defiance she'd never even have considered at the start of this evening, she ducked away before her mother could stop her and strode back to Lord Caxton, who remained alone, sipping champagne.

She took a deep breath. "Lord Caxton, I realize this is terribly forward of me," she squeaked. She cleared her throat, pushing her voice back down to her normal deeper tone. "I wonder if you might consider doing me the kindest of favors."

He nodded, his expression amused. "If it is within my power, I should be delighted."

"There is one dance remaining in the evening, and I find myself without a partner. As this is, after all, my debut, I should be most embarrassed to be a wallflower."

"Perish the thought. Although I cannot imagine a more attractive bloom, whether you are in motion or not."

Judith flushed and nearly considered abandoning this ridiculous flirtation. "Oh, my." Having exhausted her store of clever repartees, rather limited to begin with, she feverishly waved her fan in front of her face, hoping she was sending an appropriate message.

He laughed, not unkindly, and tipped her head up with a finger under her chin. "What an innocent you are. I should be delighted to dance with you." He glanced at something over her shoulder. "But we should take to the floor quickly before your mama comes back with reinforcements."

As the beginning strains of a waltz filled the air, Lord Caxton swept her onto the dance floor. He was a large man, but she was tall enough that they fit together as if two halves of a whole. He flashed a surprised grin at her, as if he were thinking the same thing. She shivered as he placed his arm around her waist, her skin tingling under his hand at the small of her back.

As they spun around the room, Judith caught glimpses of her mother on the edge of the dance floor, lips pursed tightly together, rising and falling on her toes, fists opening and closing at her side as if she were getting ready to punch someone. Judith could almost see the war between propriety and preservation taking place in her head.

The music slowed, and the waltz came to an end. Lord Caxton removed his hand from Judith's back, leaving her oddly bereft. He kissed her hand once more, bowed gracefully over it.

"Thank you for a delightful dance, Miss Leslie. I do hope we'll meet again."

"Um. Yes, thank you. I mean, you're welcome." As soon as the words left her lips, she wanted to call them back, but he was gone, his shoulders vibrating as he laughed, she was sure, at her idiotic response. She would not have been disappointed if the floor opened up and swallowed her whole.

A fate made even more attractive when her mother's talons dug into her shoulder.

"Come. With. Me." Lady Grangemore's voice was low, nearly inaudible, signaling anger so profound it didn't require words.

Judith huffed out a breath, then obediently

followed her mother to the front hall, where they bid goodnight to each remaining guest. As the last one left the house, Lady Grangemore turned to Judith.

"We will speak in the morning." She paused, held up a long finger, and shook her head. "No, the evening. I will require an entire day to overcome my desire to ship you back to Derbyshire on the mail coach."

She stalked up the stairs, leaving Judith in the hall, imprints of her mother's nails on her skin and the gentleman's hand tingling in the small of her back.

****

Peter entered the breakfast room the next morning feeling more energized than he had in months. A vision of Miss Leslie danced through his brain, the smell of her unique jasmine and rose scent still lingering in his senses. And the feel of her against him, taller than any woman with whom he'd ever danced—she'd fit within his arms as if they'd been designed for each other.

His father was hunched over the newspaper, a cup of tea at his elbow and congealing eggs on his plate.

"Morning, Father."

The earl looked up in surprise, glanced at the mantel clock, then back at Peter. "It's only nine o'clock. What's wrong?"

Peter shrugged. "Nothing is wrong. I wasn't in the mood to sleep in."

"I know very well you didn't get in until five o'clock. You tripped over the table in the upstairs hall and woke me up. Drunk, I suppose." Lord Longley grunted and returned to his paper.

"Yes, it's true, I got in quite late, but no, I wasn't drunk. You might consider leaving a lamp or two burning until I get in. It's positively tomblike upstairs after dark."

"Hmph," the earl grunted, although Peter was amused to see the hint of a smile at the corners of his father's mouth.

Peter helped himself to eggs, toast, and kippers and sat across from the earl as the footman poured his coffee. "You'll be pleased, Father, when you hear I have found a chit to court."

The paper in his father's hands twitched, but Peter was unable to see the face behind it.

"I think you'd like her, actually. She's very proper, from a good family." He took a bite of eggs. The paper twitched again, lowered ever so slightly. "Miss Judith Leslie," Peter said. "Viscount Grangemore's daughter."

The paper crashed to the table under the earl's fists. "Grangemore?" He shook his head so ferociously Peter feared it would fly off his neck. "Oh, no, lad, I could never countenance such a match. Your mother would never forgive me."

Peter paused his fork en route to his mouth. "What? What's wrong with her? And why should Mother care, especially as she's been dead for twenty years?"

"Hmph. Never you mind. Search elsewhere, my boy. Plenty of other chits out there—the Season's only just begun." He folded his paper, placed it at the side of his plate and rose, pausing to pat Peter awkwardly on the back with a curled hand. "Plenty of other chits," he muttered as he shuffled out of the room.

Feeling far less cheerful than he had when he entered the room, Peter set his fork on his plate, no longer hungry. He had thought he might actually please his father. But again, he failed.

## Chapter 3

Judith tossed and turned for much of the night, too stirred up to sleep. Her mind kept picturing Lord Caxton in his ridiculous coat, his blond hair curling where it met his collar, her hand and back still tingling where he had touched her. She had known there would be consequences for disobeying her mother and seeking out that last dance, but unless her mother deigned to tell her why he was unsuitable, she saw no reason why she couldn't satisfy her curiosity.

Finally dozing off around daybreak, she was awakened by a poke in the shoulder. "At last," her maid said, when Judith opened her eyes. "I thought you'd sleep the entire day away."

"Wha?" Judith nestled deeper into the blankets. "Go away, Grace. I didn't sleep a wink."

"There's a gentleman come to call."

"Who?"

"Lord Something-or-Other. I can't remember what Wildon said. But I peeked into the morning room. He's very handsome and exceedingly tall, with blond hair."

She sat up so abruptly she made herself a bit dizzy. Lord Caxton? "What time is it?"

"Eleven o'clock, miss."

Her stomach gave an unnerving lurch, but excitement gave way to propriety. "No gentleman would call this early, especially the day after a ball. I don't care how handsome he is. Tell Wildon to send him away."

"He tried, miss. The gentleman said he would wait."

"Well, that's ridiculous. What is my mother going to say?"

"She's gone to bed with a megrim. We won't see her for hours."

Secretly relieved she wouldn't have to worry about her mother, Judith climbed out of bed, her long legs nearly catching in the bedclothes. She stared at her wardrobe and shook her head. "Oh, Grace. What should I wear?"

Grace nearly clapped her hands with glee. Not much older than Judith herself, she was a hopeless romantic who lived for the love stories she read in the serials. A man who came to call so early in the day was a romantic story in the making.

"The green muslin, I think. It brings out the color of your eyes, miss."

Judith grinned. "Excellent choice."

Far quicker than she had ever done before, Judith was dressed and entering the morning room, Grace close behind. In a creamy white cravat and dark gray coat more subdued than the one he had worn last night, Lord Caxton stood at the window overlooking the garden. The late morning sun filtered through the glass, making his hair glow golden. He was as beautiful from behind as he was face to face.

Judith's breath hitched, and her throat went dry. "Lord Caxton," she croaked. "What an unexpected surprise."

He turned to face her, bowed. "Miss Leslie. Please

forgive my unfashionably early intrusion."

So he *was* aware of the social niceties, despite what her mother had said last night. Even if he chose to ignore them, that had to count for something.

She sat on a settee opposite the window, arranging her skirts around her. "Please, sit down, my lord." She gestured at an adjacent chair, then instructed her maid to ring for the butler.

Lord Caxton folded his enormous frame into the delicate Georgian chair. He smiled, his eyes as blue as she remembered. They made small talk until after the butler came and went, sniffing in disapproval but too well trained not to fetch them the tea and scones she requested.

"So, my lord. What brings you here at this time of the morning?"

"Will your mother not be joining us?" He surveyed the room, as if he expected Lady Grangemore to leap out from behind the drapes.

"No, she is feeling unwell this morning."

"Oh, I am sorry to hear that." He didn't appear sorry—quite the opposite. His expression had brightened as soon as Judith said her mother was ill.

"She'll be fine, I'm sure. Only a headache."

"Ah." He seemed about to say something else when Wildon returned with a tray piled high with pastries. He inserted himself between Judith and Lord Caxton, spending far longer pouring tea and arranging scones on china plates than was strictly necessary. Judith drummed her fingertips on her lap. Finally, as he turned the cups so their handles faced at a certain angle on the saucers, she could take no more.

"Thank you. That will be all, Wildon." She glared

at him, and he stared passively back. She cleared her throat, attempted to adopt her mother's occasionally fierce demeanor, but he simply stood there. "You may go."

The butler raised his beetle-black brows but said nothing. He bowed slightly and retreated. Judith suspected he went no farther than the other side of the door so he could listen to every word.

Judith was so nervous she could do no more than nibble on one of the scones. Silence stretched awkwardly between them, the only sound the ticking of the clock on the mantel. Lord Caxton sat back, one long leg crossed over the other, enjoying a pastry and studying her over the lip of his teacup.

Finally, he set down the cup. "I wanted to see you again."

Judith coughed on scone crumbs, her throat dry once more. "Why?" She picked up her tea cup and drank, her hand shaking so much she spilled some on her gown.

"Because you're delightful. You say exactly what you think. That is a rare quality in young ladies of the *ton*, I have found."

"Oh." Lord, but he made her feel stupid.

"I wondered if you might be interested in a drive in the park this afternoon."

She blinked. "In Hyde Park? With you?"

His laughter signaled her continued delightfulness. "Yes, with me, and of course in Hyde Park. Is that not where everyone will be?"

"I seldom feel the need to be where everyone is, my lord. It gets so crowded."

"True. However, I don't think your mother would

approve of us going anywhere else alone."

"Good lord, no." Judith clapped a hand to her mouth. "I mean, certainly not." But it was too late—he was laughing again, those sky-blue eyes twinkling. "To be honest, my lord, I don't think she'll approve of me going anywhere with you at all, especially when she learns you called on me this morning. She was not best pleased we shared a dance last night."

"If the daggers she was throwing at me with her eyes were any indication, I am inclined to agree with you. Perhaps it had more to do with your failing to behave like a good girl should?"

Her mouth dropped open. "I assure you, my lord, I *am* a good girl."

He cocked a brow.

She frowned. "Perhaps not last night."

He smiled a know-it-all smile.

"You're terribly annoying, did you know that?" she said, slightly exasperated.

He shrugged. "So I've been told."

"My mother does not approve of you. Why, do you think?"

"I couldn't say. Nor can I explain why my father doesn't approve of you."

"What?" Judith's eyes widened. Her maid, all but forgotten in the corner, let out a gasp, which Judith found somewhat gratifying. "But why should he disapprove of *me*? My father was a well-respected member of the peerage, God rest his soul, and my mother the very picture of propriety. And I, well, I'd never even been to London at all until three weeks ago. What could I have possibly done to make myself unsuitable?"

Lord Caxton shrugged. "It is a mystery to me as well. But I have been displeasing my father since the day I was born, so I see no reason to stop now." He rose, bowed. "Until this afternoon, Miss Leslie. I shall call for you at three o'clock."

He swept out of the room before she could refuse.

****

Peter smiled to himself as he strode out of Grangemore House, leaving the adorable Miss Leslie sputtering in confusion. He had a feeling it didn't happen often. For all her innocence, she seemed used to getting her own way. He wanted to find out why his father was so opposed to the match, and there was no better way to do that than to act in direct defiance of his wishes. Besides, he truly did find her delightful. She was the first woman he had ever met who might sway him from his inclination not to marry, and as such, he would court her no matter what her parent, or his own, might wish.

He spent the afternoon cleaning and polishing his curricle, which he had neglected for months. Leaving his father's coachman to see to the horses, he bathed and changed his clothes.

He returned to Grangemore House as the hall clock struck four. The stern butler was not pleased to see him. He opened his mouth to speak, presumably to tell him Miss Leslie was not at home, but was interrupted by the lady herself, who ducked around the servant and out the front door. Dressed in an emerald-colored riding ensemble, her glorious auburn hair piled atop her head, she was a woodland goddess.

"A curricle? Oh, how exciting! I've never been in one. Is it yours?" She ran a gloved finger over the gold trim and turned to him, her full lips slightly parted, her eyes sparkling.

"Yes, it is. I haven't used it in a while, but thought it was just the thing for a turn about the park."

"Cassandra will be green," she muttered under her breath, a happy smile playing about her lips.

"Cassandra?"

She waved a hand airily. "No one of importance. A girl I know."

"Hmm. Shall we?"

"Oh, yes." He handed her into the carriage. She arranged her skirts around her, and he caught a glimpse of a shapely ankle above a neat brown leather boot. When he sat beside her, they were nearly the same height—she had a surprisingly long torso for a woman, and she was quite tall to begin with.

He snapped the reins and the horses, a matched pair of bays, made their way the short distance to Hyde Park.

The spring day was unusually fine, and the park was crowded. The cherry trees lining the path were in full bud, their pale pink blooms filling the air with a heady fragrance. Peter wanted to engage in witty repartee with Miss Leslie, but was so out of practice with driving, he found himself occupied with trying not to hit anything.

"Do you think we might ride down Rotten Row?" Miss Leslie asked. Despite her earlier statements that she preferred to be away from the crowds, she vibrated with excitement. Her head flitted from side to side, taking in all the sights of the *ton* in full promenade. "I never have."

"I thought you didn't like crowds," Peter said.

"I don't, as a rule. But somehow it doesn't seem so bad today." She grinned at him.

"If you wish." He'd do anything she liked when she smiled in such a way. He steered the curricle toward the most popular area, hoping he could keep his bays under control.

"Oh, look! There's Cassandra," she said.

She pointed toward a sour-faced girl in a pale gold gown, her hand clutching the arm of a gentleman whose pinched expression suggested he'd rather be anywhere else. A bird of prey with a rat in her talons.

"Ah, so that's Cassandra."

"How petite and delicate she is," Miss Leslie said with a touch of bitterness. "Next to her I am such a clod. As she's never been reluctant to tell me. Her pretty face and creamy complexion hides quite a beastly personality."

Peter turned to his companion, studied her for a moment. "London is full of petite English birds, beastly and otherwise. You, my dear Miss Leslie, possess a feline grace, long and lean and utterly sensual."

She blinked her green cat eyes and stared at him. "A cat?" Peter dearly hoped he hadn't offended her. Such a remark was improper in the extreme. He opened his mouth to apologize when a sleek, satisfied smile spread across her face. "A cat. Cats eat birds for breakfast."

"That they do." They passed the beady-eyed Cassandra without saying a word. Peter glanced back to see the woman stop and stare at Miss Leslie, her face suffused with color, her brows arched, and lips pursed with fury. She tugged fiercely on her gentleman's arm and stomped off in the opposite direction.

"Do you see anyone else you'd like to chew on, my puss?"

She smiled shyly. "I am not a mean person, my lord, and I will pay dearly for cutting her just now, but she brings out the worst in me."

"She seems to have found her beau for the season."

"What?"

"The man she was with. She was clutching his arm rather possessively."

"Him?" She laughed. Not the musical titter so many debs emitted, but a full-throated sound of amusement that reverberated in his belly. "Oh no, that was her brother, Bernard. Poor man."

Poor man, indeed, although certainly not as unfortunate as the man who would eventually marry his sister.

The rest of the ride proved uneventful. He hit no one with his carriage, nor did he manage to dump Miss Leslie out of it and into the Serpentine. She proved to be an engaging companion, full of witty commentary on the people they passed. She was an observer rather than an active participant, a fact which made her all the more attractive.

Arriving at her front door, he jumped down and handed her out of the curricle. He pulled her hand toward him, brushed his lips across it, felt her tremble as they touched the soft leather of her glove. "Miss Leslie. It's been a pleasure. I hope you will ride with me again."

Her cheeks glowed pink. "I hope so too. Thank you, Lord Caxton. It was enlightening." There was a slight flutter in his belly as she moved toward the house, turned back as she reached the door. She lifted a hand, gave a slight wave and an enigmatic smile, and disappeared inside.

The flutter whirled into a storm.

## Chapter 4

"Judith, is that you? Where have you been?" Lady Grangemore called from the sitting room as Judith was handing her wrap and gloves to Wildon. Judith sighed. She wanted to return to her room to think about her glorious outing, but there was no avoiding this. God help her if the viscountess had somehow already heard about Judith's treatment of Lady Cassandra.

"Yes, Mama, I'm here. You knew I was going for a ride in the park with Lord Caxton, did you not?"

Needlepoint on her lap, a glass of sherry at her elbow, Lady Grangemore peered at Judith over her spectacles, a look cultivated to make Judith and her siblings aware she knew they'd been naughty and would suffer for it. "After I told you to have nothing to do with him? You know very well I would not have allowed it had I known."

Judith sank onto a chair. "You never told me why, Mama. He's a perfectly acceptable suitor, as far as I can tell."

"He is too old for you, and a rake to boot."

"He's not that old." She actually had no idea how old he was and had no response to the rake accusation, so she changed the subject. "The weather is lovely today, Mama. Have you gone out in the garden?"

"No, I have not, and I know what you're trying to do. You may not see him, Judith. I forbid it."

"I am nineteen, Mama. I can see whomever I like," she said, in another unusual act of defiance. Whatever was coming over her?

"No, you can't. Not if you want to live under my roof."

Judith huffed out an exasperated breath. "This is ridiculous, Mama. Please tell me what is wrong with him. Why don't you want him to court me?"

"Because he will break your heart, like his father did mine." Lady Grangemore's voice was gruff, thick with emotion.

Judith's mouth fell open in surprise. Her mother had a history with the Earl of Longley?

"What?" She moved to her mother's side, took her hands in hers. "Tell me."

Lady Grangemore's eyes glazed over as if she were staring into the past. "My debut year. Longley had inherited the title the year before, and he was so handsome. He had every deb eating out of the palm of his hand, including me. He sought me out at every ball, went riding with me in Hyde Park. We spent a lot of time together, talking. Flirting." She smiled, remembering. "He danced with me three times at Almack's, all but declaring he would offer for me. And then he disappeared for a fortnight. No one knew where he had gone, but when he came back, he was married to some red-faced Highland shrew. He never said another word to me. To this very day I don't know what happened."

Judith was quiet for a moment. What did one say to such a revelation? "I'm sorry, Mama. It must have been very painful."

Lady Grangemore released Judith's hands, wiped

away a tear. "It was. And every time you mention that man's son, it hurts all over again. Please, Judith. Stay away from him. I would spare you a similar experience."

"But it all worked out for the best, didn't it, Mama? You loved Father, didn't you?"

An awkward silence fell when the countess failed to answer right away. Finally, she shook her head, sadness coming off her in almost visible waves. "I settled for your father, truth be told. I was fond of him, yes, and he gave me three wonderful children, for which I am forever grateful. But he was not the love of my life. Longley was."

"Oh, Mama." Judith slumped back against the cushions. This revelation was worse than the first. No wonder her mother always seemed unhappy. She'd spent her entire adult life in the company of a man who couldn't make her happy, since he wasn't the one she wanted. It was unbearably sad.

She embraced her mother on an impulse, Lady Grangemore's jasmine scent curling around her nose. She held her close for a minute. "I didn't know, Mama. I'm so sorry."

Her mother hugged her back, then eased away. "You couldn't possibly have known, my dear. It was the scandal of the season, but it was thirty years ago. Nevertheless, I hope you will think about what I've said. Your season started only two days ago. You will meet plenty of other men, and I would like you to consider any one of them."

"Very well, Mama. I will."

"Good girl." Her mother patted Judith's hand. "Now go get cleaned up. We have the Greenbriar Ball this evening."

"Yes, Mama." Judith rose and went upstairs to her bedchamber, where she lay back on the bed, staring at the ceiling. She would consider other suitors, but she had a feeling she wouldn't be able to stay away from Lord Caxton, should he want to pursue her.

\*\*\*\*

Peter spent the remainder of the evening at his club, uninterested in attending two balls in as many days and unwilling to be treated to another lecture on the mysterious unsuitability of Judith Leslie. Sadly, he discovered he had merely been postponing the inevitable. The next morning at breakfast, his father informed him they would be making a call this afternoon.

"A call? On whom?"

His father did not answer the question, but fixed Peter with a glare. "Because you failed to attend to the matter of your matrimonial future with diligence, I must take this upon myself."

"What are you talking about, Father? Despite what you said yesterday, I know I have found my perfect match."

"Not Grangemore's daughter again," Lord Longley said, exasperated. "She's not at all suitable."

"Why not?"

His father exhaled slowly, every minute of his sixty-odd years etched upon his face. He rubbed a hand through his thinning hair. "Peter, is there any chance you could accept my decision on something? Just once? I do not approve of your marrying her, and that's that."

"Are you quite well, Father? You don't look it."

"No, I am not. And you haven't answered my

question."

"I don't know. Unless she's somehow your illegitimate offspring, I see no reason why you should object so strenuously."

His father winced but did not respond. He rose from the table, bones creaking. "I cannot tell you more. I shall expect you in the front hall at one o'clock. If you bear me any affection or respect, you will do as I ask."

Peter sighed. "Very well, Father. I shall be here."

"Thank you, son." He shuffled out of the room, seeming far older and more careworn than Peter had ever seen him. But Peter had no desire to stop seeing Judith Leslie. Their carriage ride the previous day had left him with a burning need to see her again. She was without doubt the only woman of his acquaintance who didn't bore him silly. And he certainly wasn't going to let his fascinating feline go without determining why.

****

As instructed, he met his father in the afternoon, and they made their way across Mayfair to the extravagant London home of the Duke of Bothwell.

"Why are we calling on Bothwell? You detest him."

"He has a daughter who has recently debuted. It would be an advantageous alliance."

"Why would he agree to such a match? She would be marrying beneath her."

"Not by much, and His Grace is severely short of funds. He needs to marry her to a titled man of means, and quickly. There is a distinct shortage of marriageable dukes and marquesses this year."

It was at times like these that Peter was all too clear on why Society called the Season "the marriage mart."

He felt like a horse at market. He bared his lips over gritted teeth. "Shall I show him my teeth?"

The earl frowned, his dark brows coming together in a single busy line. "Don't be impertinent, Peter. In a man of your years, it's a most irritating trait."

Peter forbore from further comment, impertinent or otherwise. They passed Grangemore House, and he peered out of the carriage window just as Judith and her mother emerged from the front door, chatting animatedly. Beside him, his father stiffened and leaned back, as if he didn't want to be seen.

Peter glanced from his father to Lady Grangemore and back. Perhaps there was something there—the earl was roughly the same age as Lady Grangemore. Perhaps his adverse response to Judith had far more to do with her mother than with the girl herself. He stowed the information in the back of his brain for later review.

All too soon, they had arrived at the Bothwells' residence. It was a magnificent Georgian structure, built less than a century before. It was ostentatious in the extreme—the Dukes of Bothwell had ever been ones to wear their wealth on their sleeves—and just walking through the heavy front doors made Peter itchy.

They were led into a sitting room that immediately stung Peter's eyes. From the drapes to the walls to the painfully busy Oriental rug, every surface was covered in gold. Peter had never seen anything quite so ugly in his life.

His discomfort only grew at the sight of the young woman his father wanted him to meet: Lady Cassandra from the day before. She resembled even more the bird of prey today, dressed in a rust-colored gown with a feathery headdress perched atop her blonde hair. Her eyes widened when she saw him, then narrowed as if he were her next meal. It clearly had not escaped her that he was the man in the curricle with Judith, a woman who had all but delivered Lady Cassandra a cut direct.

"My lord," she said, dipping into a respectful curtsy. "It is a pleasure to make your acquaintance. I believe we may have seen each other before, however."

"The pleasure is mine, my lady, although I don't believe we've met before." He bowed over her hand. He had not told his father he'd gone out with Miss Leslie. He prayed Lady Cassandra would not pursue the subject further, but her expression bore a resemblance to the greedy, slightly fierce expression of a dog with a meaty bone, and he doubted she would let it go for long.

"Please do sit, my lords," Cassandra's mother, Lady Bothwell, said. They perched uncomfortably on a delicate settee designed more for appearance than for comfort, especially for a pair of gentlemen of their size. Lady Bothwell's gaze traveled down Peter's body and then up again, lingering on his groin as if she were calculating his physical prowess.

"How are you enjoying the season, Lord Caxton?" Lady Bothwell asked. "I have not seen you at many soirees thus far."

"I hope to attend many of them, Your Grace. In fact, I hope you will save me a dance at your own ball tomorrow evening?" He flashed his most charming smile, which had the desired effect and halted further questions. The woman simpered and waved a well-manicured hand in the air.

"I would be delighted, but you should save that dance for Cassandra."

He'd rather choke, but he said, "Of course. Lady Cassandra, will you put me on your dance card?"

"Certainly, Lord Caxton." She leaned back slightly in her seat and fixed her gaze upon him. "I believe you are acquainted with Miss Judith Leslie?"

"Yes, we have met," he said cautiously. This visit was about to go badly awry.

"Now *was* it you I saw driving her about in the park yesterday? You do look *so* like that gentleman." Before he could respond, she waved her hand in an exact mimic of her mother. "Oh, but it couldn't have been. *You* would certainly never countenance such rude behavior."

His father and Lady Bothwell turned as one to glare at him.

"I am terribly sorry, Lady Cassandra, but although I did ride with Miss Leslie in Hyde Park yesterday, I am unaware of rudeness on anyone's part. Miss Leslie did not mention you," he lied. "I can only assume she did not see you, or surely she would have greeted you. She is a most correct young lady."

"Hmph." Judging from her pinched expression, Lady Cassandra was unimpressed with his response. She could not directly contradict a gentleman, however, even one she knew was lying, without being accused of the very rudeness she sought to condemn.

"His lordship must be right, Cassandra. She must not have seen you," her mother said, dismissing the entire incident.

Peter avoided his father's eye for the duration of the excruciating interview. For all her beauty, Lady Cassandra was every bit the nasty shrew Miss Leslie had suggested. He'd rather join a monastery than marry her.

In the carriage afterwards, Lord Longley turned to him. "You neglected to tell me you'd gone driving with Miss Leslie."

"I was unaware I was required to share my schedule with you. We were in my curricle, open for all to see. No declarations were made, and nothing untoward occurred."

"I don't recall accusing you of impropriety, Peter. I merely wondered why you hadn't told me."

"Because I knew it would upset you. As it obviously has."

His father took a deep breath then changed the subject. "What did you think of Lady Cassandra?"

"Do you want my honest opinion?"

"Of course," the earl said. Peter refrained from saying he'd never asked for it before.

"I think she's a shrew who'd make her husband's life a living hell."

The earl uttered a cough-laugh. "Perhaps not that honest."

Peter shrugged. "You asked. Besides, I doubt very much she'll have me. Miss Leslie all but gave her the cut direct yesterday, and she knows I know it."

"So you lied to her today?"

"Of course I did. It would have been rude to do otherwise."

"I suppose, but it was badly done. You may be correct about Lady Cassandra's inclination, but unfortunately..." He paused, wearing the same somber expression a doctor would use to tell a man he was dying. "...the duke and I have already agreed on terms."

Peter's jaw dropped. "You did what?"

"You will marry Lady Cassandra in two weeks' time."

His gut lurched, the cucumber sandwiches he'd eaten at the Bothwells' threatening to make a return appearance. He bit back the bile in his throat. "I don't believe this. How could you? I'm no pimple-faced lad you can order about!"

"I'm sorry, Peter. Had I known how much you'd dislike her, I would never have agreed to the match, but unless she rejects you after today's meeting, the deed is done."

Peter threw up his arms, nearly taking off his father's head in the process. "But what about what I want? Did you never consider that?"

The earl tried a placating tone. "I didn't think you cared one way or the other. And I certainly didn't think you'd react so strongly."

"You told me I had to start courting. Why did you say that if you'd already agreed to marry me off?"

His father was obviously losing patience, his eyes narrowing and his face turning red. "I hadn't already agreed to marry you off. The duke called on me unexpectedly that afternoon."

There weren't enough words in the English language to fully express Peter's outrage and dismay. He was to throw over Miss Leslie for Cassandra? He couldn't bear it. "What about Miss Leslie? What is so wrong with her that you choose this path for me as an alternative?"

His father was quiet for a moment. "I have a history with her mother. It did not end well."

Peter sat back in the carriage and stared at his

father. "What does that mean?"

"I all but promised to marry her, and then, well, I was forced to marry your mother."

"Why?"

The earl's shoulders hunched, and he looked away. "Because I had ruined her."

Peter stiffened. "You ruined Mother?"

His father stared into the distance, suddenly lost in memory. "She visited Longley Hall during a country weekend, and we had a dalliance. One of those things, caught up in the moment, and all that. She was, shall we say, experienced in such matters. It was all in good fun; she was promised to another and wanted an adventure before she settled down. Or so she said."

Peter shook his head. "Good God. Stop, please." The very idea of his sainted mother, a woman of loose morals.

His father ignored him, as if now he had started relating the tale he didn't dare stop. "She returned to Scotland. I traveled to London and proceeded to look for a wife. Within weeks I had found one, in Miss Leslie's mother, Lady Margaret. I was prepared to offer for her, but before I could do so, I was summoned back to Durham and confronted with a newly enceinte Lady Constance MacNevan and her irate father.

"We had to marry, obviously. And I never spoke to Margaret again."

Peter's brain reeled, trying to understand how his parents could have done such a thing. He slumped against the side of the carriage. "I had no idea."

The earl laughed without a trace of mirth. "How could you? It is not something one tells one's children. And if the *ton* noticed you were born a mere seven months after we married, no one spoke of it. At least not in my hearing."

Peter was silent for a moment, listening to the clip clop of the horses on the pavement below them. Finally he said, "Do you regret marrying Mother?" He remembered the conversation they'd had a few days before.

"I will always regret hurting Margaret. But your mother was pleasant enough, I suppose, and we always got on well in the bedchamber."

The sandwiches flipped in his gut again. "Oh, God," he groaned. "Please don't say any more."

Lord Longley chuckled, in better spirits now he'd disgorged his appalling tale. "In any case, your mother was terribly jealous of Margaret, because she knew I had been in love with her and suspected I never stopped. It would displease her greatly were you to marry her daughter."

"She's dead, Father. She is well past caring."

"It matters not, my boy. Neither of us had the life we wanted. I owe her that much."

Peter sighed. "That's ridiculous, Father. She would want me to be happy."

"Perhaps. Nevertheless, you will abide by my wishes, and marry Lady Cassandra."

It was useless to argue further, at least for now. The rest of the way home he stared out the window, seeing nothing but a curl of auburn hair framing gorgeous green eyes.

## Chapter 5

Although she didn't disobey her mother and seek out Lord Caxton, Judith couldn't stop herself from watching for him at every ball and soiree. She had fully expected to see him at the Bothwells' ball, but Cassandra, with an annoyingly knowing air, had said he was indisposed and had sent his regrets.

Every knock upon her front door raised her hopes he had come to call, but she was constantly disappointed. She wondered whether his father had forbidden him to see her. Did Lord Longley even remember jilting her mother? Did he regret it? If they had married, neither she nor Lord Caxton would exist at all. And she certainly wouldn't be mooning over him.

Her mind continued to turn over these random thoughts as she danced with Lord Dimsdale at his sister's ball. He was nearly a head shorter than she, and she had to continually remind herself not to lead.

"It's a lovely party, whot?" he said to her breasts as he twirled her around the floor.

"Yes, it is." As it wasn't difficult to see over his head, she idly monitored the entrance to the room.

"Excuse me, Dimmy, but would you mind if I cut in?" A pair of strong arms pulled her away from Lord Dimsdale, who sputtered in ineffectual protest.

"He was drooling over your perfect bosom, my dear," Lord Caxton said after he'd taken her in his arms. "I'm surprised your bodice isn't soaked with spittle."

She barely had time to register his presence before he'd spun her toward the edge of the floor. When the music stopped, they strolled out onto the terrace. It was nearly empty of people since the evening was unseasonably cool. The few who were there melted into the shadows, far more concerned with each other than with Judith and Lord Caxton.

"When did you arrive? I..." She refused to tell him she'd been watching for him. "I didn't know you were expected."

"I've been in the card room," he said. He leaned against the balustrade and regarded her with hooded eyes.

"All evening?"

"Why? Were you hoping I'd make an appearance?" He grinned.

"Certainly not. I've barely spared you a thought since we last met."

He held a hand to his chest. "You wound me, truly you do."

"At least you're wearing a fashionable waistcoat today," she said with a sniff.

He laughed. "My, my. Feeling feisty today, are you?"

She *was* feisty. And so irritated with him for not calling upon her again, even though she wasn't supposed to see him at all. "Perhaps," she said, more slyly than she planned.

"I think you were watching for me after all." He studied her, and when she didn't respond, said, "I am sorry I didn't call after our drive in the park. I had some…family obligations. I assure you it was not lack of interest on my part."

"I hadn't noticed." She brushed a stray curl from her cheek and attempted a neutral expression.

"I need to tell you something. Something I'd prefer you didn't hear from someone else."

Her curiosity piqued, she considered him. His lips were set into a grim line, but as he gazed into her eyes his features softened. His lips parted, and he leaned forward. "I…"

She was mesmerized. "You wanted to tell me something?" she said, a trifle breathless. She brushed an imaginary hair off her face.

"Did I?" he murmured, then pressed his lips to hers. She quivered at the touch of his hand at the small of her back, the other gently massaging the nape of her neck. He pushed closer, parting her lips with his tongue. She closed her eyes, allowed him to deepen the kiss. He tasted of whisky, smelled of sandalwood soap. Her hands moved of their own accord around his neck. She grabbed fistfuls of his thick hair and held on as he plundered her mouth.

He pulled away and she gasped for air, as if she couldn't breathe without him. She moaned, her eyes fluttering open.

"I'm…" he started, but she silenced him with her mouth. After a moment, she pulled away.

Her eyes returned to focus, registered his guilty expression. She shook her head. "If you say you're sorry, I shall smack you. You're not sorry at all, and neither am I."

He pressed his forehead against hers. "No, I'm not sorry. Not about kissing you, at any rate."

"What were you going to tell me?"

He didn't answer but kissed her again, and it was some glorious moments before they again broke apart.

"You're trying to distract me," she whispered.

"Is it working?" She felt his smile against her lips.

"Yes. But we've been out here for too long. We should go inside before we're missed."

"I prefer it here. In this spot, this time. Nothing but you, and me." He nuzzled her neck. She backed behind a potted plant, shielding them further from view. Her breasts tingled as his mouth made damp circles on her skin.

She tilted her head to give him greater access, even as one part of her heated brain realized they had to stop. "Lord Caxton, we…"

"Shh." His mouth again found hers, and it took every ounce of restraint not to jump into his arms and wrap her legs around his waist.

Murmured voices from the other side of the plant caused them both to straighten. Judith held her breath, waiting for the other couple to pass. Fortunately, Lord Caxton's magnificent frame completely hid her. It had never happened before—it was wonderful to be embraced by a man who was taller than she was. She also had never been kissed, like that or otherwise, and her knees were weak.

She adjusted her fichu and patted her hair, hoping nothing was out of place. "We must go in, my lord. We'll be found out."

"Would that be so bad?"

She eyed him with confused surprise. "Are you honestly asking if I would mind you ruining my reputation?"

He sighed, his expression one of acute disappointment. "Of course not. I wouldn't do such a thing to you. But I don't want this to end."

"Lord Caxton?"

"Peter."

"What?"

"I think you should call me Peter now, don't you?"

Her cheeks warmed as she remembered, but she pushed the thought away and focused on what she wanted to ask him.

"Peter, then. I wondered, did your father tell you not to see me?"

He was quiet for a moment, his face shadowed in the flickering light from the ballroom. "Yes."

"Did he tell you why?"

"Yes. Although I suspect it's not quite the same story your mother gave you. This is where this conversation is headed, is it not?"

"What did he tell you?"

"That, my darling, is a question I am not at liberty to answer quite yet."

"But—" A door opened and a woman emerged from the ballroom. Her silhouette was all too familiar. Judith groaned. "Oh, no, it's my mother. Stay here."

Judith pushed Peter back into the shadows and came out from behind the plant. She leaned forward on the balustrade, as if she'd been studying the topiary in the garden for the last hour, or however long they'd been out there.

"There you are," Lady Grangemore said. "I've been looking for you an age. Have you been out on the terrace all this time?"

Judith turned and smiled innocently. Or at least she

hoped it was innocent. "Oh, hello, Mama. It was stifling in there, so I came out for air. It's such a beautiful evening."

Her mother raised her eyebrows. "It's cold, and you've missed two dances, Judith. People are beginning to talk. Come quickly, or you'll miss the last waltz on top of everything else."

Her mother clutched Judith's elbow and steered her inside. She risked a quick glimpse over her shoulder, but if Peter was still there, he was skilled at hiding.

\*\*\*\*

Peter couldn't enter the ballroom from the terrace after Judith returned; he'd heard her mother say she'd been missed, and if Lady Grangemore saw him, she'd know instantly they'd been together. Despite what he'd said, it would be bad indeed if it were even hinted she'd been out there with him. Especially because in two days' time his engagement to Lady Cassandra would be announced. He'd meant to tell Judith. He had opened his mouth to speak, but when she'd focused those lovely green eyes on him he'd been lost. Wholly, utterly lost. So he'd kissed her.

Afterwards he knew he'd never be able to marry Lady Cassandra. He would go against his father's wishes and marry the woman he was coming to love. He just had to figure out how to do it without ruining them both.

## Chapter 6

As usual after an encounter with Lord Caxton, Judith found it impossible to sleep. She spent half the night staring in her bedchamber mirror, touching her lips and sighing, and the other half gazing at the silky fabric topping her four poster bed, imagining what it would be like to be his wife.

Plans for convincing her mother she should be permitted to marry him floated aimlessly through her brain, fleeing like a cat in a bathtub every time she remembered Peter had not actually proposed. If he was the rake Lady Grangemore claimed he was, perhaps he was simply toying with her.

But that kiss—kisses—hadn't felt playful.

She had finally dropped off to sleep close to dawn, what seemed only moments before her maid came in to wake her, bearing a cup of chocolate and a devastated expression.

"What's wrong?" Judith sat up straight, expecting to hear her mother was ill.

"Oh, miss." Grace shook her head, her expression morphing into pity.

"Out with it, please. You know I hate suspense."

"You've not read the paper this morning, then?"

Judith narrowed her eyes. "You just woke me. I have never been in the habit of reading the newspaper in my sleep, assuming I read it at all."

Grace sighed dramatically. Judith refrained from shaking her, although she dearly wanted to do so.

"It's Lord Caxton, miss. I'm sorry to tell you, but..."

Lady Grangemore burst in before she could finish her sentence. Glancing sharply at Grace, who disappeared with surprising haste along with Judith's breakfast, her ladyship sat on the edge of Judith's bed and took her hand.

Judith began to worry in earnest now—her mother never rose before noon, let alone tread the halls in her nightgown. Was Lord Caxton hurt? Killed in that curricle of his? Oh, God.

"Mama? Would someone please tell me what is going on? Peter's dead, isn't he? I know it!" A tear leaked out of the corner of her eye.

Her mother raised an eyebrow, probably at Judith's use of Lord Caxton's Christian name, then shook her head. "Dead? Where on earth did you get that idea? No, he's very much alive, and far more like his father than I would have expected. He's engaged, Judith. To Cassandra Bothwell. It was announced in *The Times* today." She held out the newspaper, carefully folded to display the announcement.

Judith's mind reeled. Engaged?

Engaged!

He had to have been engaged to the woman he knew she detested when he kissed her last night. She spared a quick moment for the thought he had been trying to tell her something but pushed it away in the face of his enormous betrayal.

"No. It can't possibly be true." She snatched the paper out of her mother's hands and read it carefully. It was all there, in black and white. Lord Caxton, heir to the Earl of Longley, to marry Cassandra, daughter of the Duke of Bothwell. Judith closed her eyes to block the image from her view, but the words swam in front of her. Her stomach roiled as the realization set in.

"I'm sorry, darling," her mother whispered.

Pain stabbed at her heart, run through by an invisible sword. Judith's eyes flew open. "No, you're not. You told me to stay away from him, and I didn't. Now my heart is broken and you feel justified, knowing you were right all along." Tears streamed unchecked. She rubbed a fist angrily across her cheeks.

"That's not fair, Judith. I never wanted this. I forbid you to see him precisely so he wouldn't break your heart."

Judith slid down into the bedclothes, turned away. "Please leave me, Mama. I need to be alone."

There was silence for a moment. Her mother leaned over and kissed the top of her head, patted her shoulder, and left, the door softly closing behind her.

Judith's tears dried; she was too angry now. She wished she could decide with whom she was angriest—him, or herself.

\*\*\*\*

"It's in *The Times*? Father, how could you? You were supposed to wait two days. I haven't had a chance to tell her yet." His father handed him the paper without comment to confirm the awful truth.

Peter stared at the announcement, as if his desperate wish would cause the words to vanish from the page. The words he had left unspoken last night now threatened to choke him.

What must she be thinking?

He threw the paper to the table and rose.

"Where are you going?" his father asked.

"To see Judith. To explain."

"Don't be ridiculous. As usual, you're allowing your emotions to get in the way of your good sense. Assuming you have any, of course," the earl muttered.

"At least I have emotions." Peter cast a withering glare at his father, barely registering the fall of the older man's face before he turned and left the room. His statement was hurtful, but this entire mess was the earl's fault. Once he'd extricated himself from this unwanted alliance with Bothwell and secured Judith's hand, he would make amends with his father.

Maybe.

Unfortunately, however, Grangemore's stern-faced butler would not admit him, no matter how charmingly he begged. He stood on the steps of the house after his fourth unsuccessful attempt to gain admittance and scanned the windows. Was it his imagination, or did one of the curtains twitch?

He was preparing to walk around to the back of the house to seek entry through the kitchen when a voice addressed him.

"She doesn't want to see you." Lady Grangemore's head emerged from an open window. Peter couldn't imagine how angry a viscountess would have to be to hang out the window like a common strumpet.

"I want her to know I'm sorry. I tried to tell her last night, but..." Telling her how her daughter's lips distracted him probably wouldn't help his cause. "It wasn't my doing, and I have no intention of marrying that vicious creature. Will you tell her?"

"I'll do nothing of the kind, and you will marry—

what did you call her?"

"A…"

Lady Grangemore waved a hand in dismissal. "Never mind. You will do your duty, of course, like your father before you, regardless of who you hurt in the process. We will be leaving Town until the deed is done. I do not expect to see you here again, Caxton."

She shut the window with a decisive thud and flicked the drapes closed.

He stood on the street, unaffected by the jostling of passersby as her words echoed in his ears.

Leaving Town? Going where?

Home? Country house party?

A house party was more likely; traveling all the way back to Derbyshire, a three day journey, would be a social defeat he did not imagine Lady Grangemore was willing to concede.

Something niggled at the back of his brain. He took a last look at the windows, imagining a sad green eye peering out at him, and went home to find an invitation.

****

"Why are we going to a house party? In Kent, of all places? The Season just began." Judith was perilously close to whining, but she couldn't seem to help herself. She curled in a chair by the window, while Grace packed a fortnight's worth of clothing under Lady Grangemore's scrutiny.

"There's a terrible outbreak of cholera that's beginning to spread to Mayfair," her mother said, notably avoiding Judith's eyes. "Lady Howley is offering a respite until it is contained."

"This is the first time you have so much as mentioned this, Mama. It's an excuse, not a reason.

You just don't want me to see Lord Caxton."

"You don't want to see him either." Lady Grangemore studied Judith. "Do you?"

"Of course not," she snapped, wondering if she meant it.

"This will eliminate the chances you will encounter him accidentally, which would be terribly awkward and invite gossip. By the time we return, he will be wed to Lady Cassandra and you can proceed with the Season."

The pain in Judith's heart settled into a dull but persistent ache. "Very well."

She stared morosely out the window, wishing he would return. She knew he'd exchanged words with her mother—Grace had seen Lady Grangemore slamming the drawing room window shut—but no one would tell Judith what he'd said. The likelihood she would never see him again, kiss him again, was uncomfortably high. An unintentional sigh—more of a moan, really— escaped her lips.

"Oh, enough, Judith," Lady Grangemore muttered to the ceiling.

Her mother should have been more sympathetic, given the parallels between her own situation and Judith's, but instead the woman was all business. She directed Grace to close the trunk and ring for a footman.

"Come. We'll have tea and then set out. It would be nice to get at least halfway by nightfall."

There was a pause, and Lady Grangemore moved to Judith's side, placing a gentle hand on her shoulder. "Come along, darling. I know you're upset, but this will pass. Howley House is quite an impressive pile, I'm told, and there are tunnels for smugglers underneath."

Judith cocked her brow. "Smugglers? Why are you using that as an enticement and not telling me to stay away?"

"Because I know very well you and your brothers used to play pirate when you were young. And because I expect the smugglers are long gone. It would be perfectly safe to explore. Perhaps I'll even join you."

Judith couldn't stop a tiny smile from forming as she imagined her mother exploring dark and musty smugglers' tunnels, brushing cobwebs from her eyes.

Lady Grangemore seized on it, of course. "Ha. I knew that would cheer you. Now, time for tea. I'm famished."

Judith allowed herself to be hauled to her feet and dragged downstairs, sparing one last glance toward the window and the future she might have had with the beautiful man in the ridiculous waistcoat.

## Chapter 7

It didn't take long for Peter to determine there were house parties taking place in Surrey and Kent over the next fortnight, and that he had been invited to both. A visit to his club in the evening for a chat with the most gossipy man in London yielded information on which party Lady Grangemore planned to attend. He penned a note of acceptance to Lady Howley, who was, conveniently, his godmother and instructed his valet to pack a trunk.

Before he could leave, however, he needed to talk to his intended. Perhaps she could be persuaded to break the engagement.

Needing to clear his head, he walked to the Bothwells' townhouse. The butler eagerly admitted him when he provided his name, despite the fact he was calling unfashionably early—apparently a new habit for him. He was asked to wait in the morning room, another garish, cluttered chamber evidencing Lady Bothwell's unfortunate taste for gilt. It did open out onto a lovely garden, however, which Peter found preferable to look upon.

The door opened with a soft snick, and he turned to greet Lady Cassandra. She swept into the room, leaving the door slightly ajar. She wore a pale blue morning gown that did little for her complexion. Her blonde hair was piled atop her head, delicate curls bouncing beside her ears. She was pretty, it was true, but she was not striking. Beside Judith, she was a mere bauble.

With such ungenerous thoughts pushing into his brain, he bowed and kissed her hand. It was rather a long way down; she was a tiny thing who barely came up to his chest. "Lady Cassandra."

"Lord Caxton," she said, gesturing to a chair before sitting opposite, "to what do I owe this pleasure?"

"I apologize for my early call, Lady Cassandra, but I wanted to discuss something with you."

"Really? And what might that be?"

"Considering we had never met before our parents arranged this match, I wondered how you felt about it."

Her eyes narrowed. "I will assume by your question you are not in favor of it?"

"The truth is my heart belongs to another. It doesn't seem fair to either of us to marry, given that fact."

"Miss Leslie, I suppose?" She sniffed.

"It would be ungallant to share her name."

"I suppose so." Disappointment, presumably at being deprived gossip, flashed across her face before it assumed its usual pinched expression. "No, Lord Caxton, I am not overjoyed at the match. You are beneath me, after all."

"The daughter of a duke is only one rank above a countess. I won't be that far beneath you, once I inherit the earldom." Peter knew Debrett's as well as she did.

She sneered at him, her beauty all but disappearing as her true nature shone through. "But in the meantime, I'd be a viscountess, wouldn't I? A far cry from a duke's daughter."

Hope filled Peter's breast. "So you agree to call off

the engagement?"

She sneered. "Don't be ridiculous. My father would kill me. You may be of lower rank, but your estate has pots of money. I'd be a fool to refuse your suit without any other options."

He tamped down his irritation and seized upon the last part of her statement. "So if you had another option, you would throw me over?"

She smiled, the kind of predatory grimace he imagined one might see on a jackal. "Without hesitation, my lord. Find me an acceptable duke or marquess, and you can marry your horsey Miss Leslie with my blessing."

His annoyance and disgust with this arrogant creature threatened to overpower him. He would find her another suitor, even if he had to pay someone to marry her.

But he didn't let it show. "I will see what I can do," he said. "I'm leaving shortly for a house party, which I suspect will have an eligible gentleman or two in attendance. May we postpone our blessed event for a month while I make my inquiries?"

She nodded. "Of course. I am sure I can convince my father. I do need to have an entire trousseau made, after all." She rose and held out a hand, dismissing him.

He dutifully kissed it, feeling an overwhelming need to wash afterwards. But at least she had given him a way out.

"Goodbye, my lord. I look forward to meeting your replacement. I shall pretend to be furious you have left Town. It will be make it easier for me to cry off when you have fulfilled your end of the bargain."

"Goodbye, Lady Cassandra. I am sure I will find

someone suitable in no time."

****

He remained in London for the rest of the day, although he itched to go after Judith. He needed to arrive after the Leslies, which would make it too awkward for them to turn around and leave once his presence was known. He had asked his godmother not to tell anyone of his planned attendance, so there would be no risk Lady Grangemore would change her mind; at least not on his account.

After spending a sleepless night coming up with a depressingly short list of eligible suitors for Cassandra, he left his father a note saying he had gone to the country and set off for Kent. Finding a new suitor would accomplish nothing if he could not convince Judith to forgive him—and to convince her mother to allow his suit.

It was a long but pleasant ride to the southeast. The approach to Howley House was fairly spectacular. The home featured a graceful arched entryway flanked by bays full of windows, topped by Dutch gables undulating like waves from the sea beyond it. On a stormy day, he imagined it would be dark and imposing with a backdrop of blue-black clouds, but now the sun shone brightly, nary a cloud in the sky, and the blue-green water of the Channel behind the house was calm. A breeze lifted the hair off his neck, smelling of the lilacs flanking the house and the faint fishy odor he always associated with the coast.

He tied his horse to the post at the front of the house and knocked. "Good afternoon," he said when the door creaked open in front of a tall, slender butler. "I am Lord Caxton. I believe I am expected."

The butler nodded. "Very good, my lord. Your valet arrived a short while ago." He gestured to a footman to see about Peter's horse, then led Peter into a medieval entry hall with a magnificent mahogany staircase. The banister was carved with faces and ornate curves, the posts topped with some sort of large cat, each in a slightly different attack pose. Peter couldn't shake the feeling the faces were watching him—and laughing—as he followed the butler upstairs.

"I've placed you in the gentlemen's wing, my lord," the man said. "There's a view of the labyrinth with the sea beyond." He stopped at the end of the corridor and opened the door. Windows extended nearly from floor to ceiling. The sea stretched out in front of him, making it feel as if he would tumble into it if he moved any closer. He couldn't recall ever seeing anything quite like it. "I trust it will suit?" the butler said.

"Yes, this will do nicely, Thank you, ...?"

"Mears, my lord."

"Ah. Thank you, Mears. Has the rest of the party arrived?"

"Yes, my lord. You are the last of the guests to arrive," he said with a sniff. "Lady Howley will greet guests at seven in the parlor. Dinner will be served promptly at eight. If you ring, one of the footmen will escort you."

"I'm sure I can find my own way, thank you, Mears."

"Very good, my lord." The man sniffed again and glowered down his prominent nose before leaving Peter alone. It was clear what he thought of Peter's navigational abilities.

He strolled to the windows and gazed out at the magnificent view. As Mears had mentioned, there was a large labyrinth below. At its center a fountain was surrounded by potted plants with vibrant flowers, and a single wrought iron bench. A hatless figure sat upon it, feet curled under her, reading a book. She turned her head, and the sunlight danced upon her fiery hair.

Judith.

Butterflies danced in his belly at the sight of her.

As if sensing his regard, she tilted her head up shielding her eyes with one hand, but after a moment returned to her book. He hoped it was because she couldn't see him, and not because she was indifferent. He'd defied his father, traveled seventy-five miles, and subjected himself to the dullness of a country house party—all for her. Indifference would be difficult to bear.

He took a moment to study the pattern of the labyrinth before setting out to conquer it.

And the woman within.

****

Judith's skin itched with the sensation she was being watched. It was highly likely—the house was absolutely covered in windows, and it certainly shouldn't surprise her that someone might be looking out at the magnificent gardens. But every time she glanced at the building, she could see nothing—the glare from the sun made all those windows opaque.

She attempted to concentrate on her book, a relatively new one about a ship and pirates and a mutiny, or something. It wasn't quite her cup of tea, but it had been the first thing she'd seen in the library on her way out of doors.

The day was glorious—cloudless sky, brilliant sun, the scent of lilacs nearly overpowering. Her mother, and presumably the rest of the guests, was resting after their journey, which though tedious had been entirely uneventful. Judith had been far too tired of sitting in the carriage even to think of resting. When she'd spotted the labyrinth and its adorable fountain in the center from her room, she'd known exactly where she wanted to spend the afternoon.

After a walk to stretch her cramped legs, she'd made her way to the bench and opened her book, but thoughts of Lord Caxton swirled through her mind, distracting her. Now she gave up and set the book down, then uncurled her feet from beneath her bottom. Closing her eyes, she arched her back, enjoying the stretch of her muscles and the warmth of the sun on her face. Her mother would be terribly cross that she'd gone out without a bonnet or a parasol, but even if her face freckled, it would be worth it for these few moments of peaceful warmth.

"Are you enjoying your patch of sunshine, little cat?"

Judith jumped, her eyes flying open. "Peter!" He stood at the entrance to the clearing, gazing down at her with a tender but apprehensive expression. Joy at seeing him warred with anger. She was still trying to decide which would prevail when he sat beside her.

"Hello, Judith." He took one of her hands in his and laid a kiss across her knuckles. She shuddered at the touch then tugged her hand from his grasp.

"What are you doing here?"

"You wouldn't see me in London, so I followed you here."

"Followed?" She scooted away a bit. It was disconcerting to be so close to him.

"Not literally, of course. But your mother had mentioned you were going to the country, and it was not hard to deduce your destination."

"I see," she said, although she didn't. "Why?"

"Do you really need to ask?" His gaze bored into her own. She blinked to break the spell and rose, walking away from him. If she didn't get away from him, she'd forget how angry she was and focus on the little thrill that curled around her belly when she thought about him chasing after her.

She pushed the thrill away, concentrated on the anger instead. "Obviously I do. You kissed me, all but declared your intention to offer for me. But the next morning I read you are engaged to someone else. Cassandra, of all people. How could you?"

"It was not my doing, I swear it. My father arranged it without my knowledge. I have no intention of marrying her."

She turned to face him. Hope swelled within her breast. "So you didn't know you were engaged when you kissed me?"

A shadow fell over his face, and he did not reply.

Of course he had known. Her blood warmed and her hands clenched involuntarily. "Did you know when we went riding in the park? Or was that solely meant to embarrass me and your fiancée?"

"No!" He rose, closed the distance between them. "No, I didn't. I wasn't engaged then. It was all arranged by my father, and I didn't learn about it until after we met. And I meant to tell you at the ball, but I... There was moonlight, and you're so beautiful, and I..."

Placing his enormous hands on her shoulders, he bent his head to kiss her again. His lips moved closer. She could smell the sweetness of tea on his breath, feel the warmth of his body as he pressed it closer to hers.

"No," she groaned, sliding from his grasp and moving away. She shook her head. "No, no, no. I'll not fall for that again." She pivoted to put him out of her sight and ran headlong into the labyrinth.

## Chapter 8

"Damn it," Peter muttered as Judith's skirts swirled and disappeared into the hedge. He had not thought it would be difficult to win her over, had assumed her mother was his biggest obstacle.

He was an ass.

He had hurt her far worse than he realized, and she was not going to let him back into her heart easily.

Should he follow her? What if she was so upset she got lost?

He swore to himself again and plunged into the hedge after her.

He needn't have worried. In the time he'd spent dithering over whether to follow her, she had escaped the maze and was nearly at the house when he caught sight of her. She didn't once turn back to see if he followed her. Did that mean she didn't care, or that she assumed he would?

He lengthened his stride to reach her but stopped short when her mother met her at the door. He ducked out of sight behind a fish-shaped topiary. There would be time enough for that confrontation.

\*\*\*\*

The nerve of him! To assume she'd welcome his advances when he was engaged to another? What kind of woman did he think she was? Indignation, and fear that she might give in, fueled every step propelling her to the house. After leaving the maze, she could feel his eyes on her back, but she dare not turn.

Her mother's figure filled the doorway as she approached, concern and annoyance on her face. "There you are!" she said. "You seem flushed, darling. Where on earth have you been?"

Judith paused, willing her breathing to slow. "I went for a walk and found a delightful little garden in the center of the labyrinth. I was reading."

"Oh, Judith," she said, shaking her head. "You went for a walk with a book?"

"Of course. I always do, or have you forgotten?" Judith usually did have a book in hand when walking at their estate in Derbyshire. Her mother always fretted she'd trip over a tree root by not watching where she was going, but it hadn't happened yet.

"No, I haven't," her mother said, disappointment tinging her tone. "I had hoped you'd eschew that country habit for this party, but clearly it's too well ingrained. But where is your book?"

"Right..." Judith realized she must have left it on the bench, she'd been so flustered by Lord Caxton's appearance. She was not about to tell her mother that, however. "Oh. I must have left it on the bench. I will get it later."

Lady Grangemore waved a beringed hand. "I'll send a footman. Now, come," she said, wrapping an arm around Judith's shoulder, "you'll never guess who's arrived."

"I can't imagine." She risked a quick glance behind her, but if Peter was there he was well hidden. She accompanied her mother into the small library from which she'd liberated the book, with lovely large windows facing the sea. She sat beside her mother and readied herself.

"Lord Kingsley," Lady Grangemore said. "A duke, for goodness' sake, and rather a handsome one at that. His mother debuted with Lady Howley, and like the rest of us, they've come to Kent to escape the cholera. What luck!"

"For whom? Surely not the people who are suffering from cholera, assuming they exist."

Her mother actually rolled her eyes. "Foolish girl. Of course it's not lucky for them, but it *is* lucky for us. You'll have an opportunity to charm him you would not otherwise have, competing with the likes of Cassandra."

The thought of Cassandra and her preening, hateful ways filled Judith's mouth with bile. The thought of her with Lord Caxton almost made it spill over. She shuddered, swallowed, took a deep breath.

"Cassandra is taken, if you'll recall."

"Hmph," Lady Grangemore muttered. "I've heard Lord Caxton has left London."

"Really? How curious." She traced the pattern on the arm of the settee with one finger. "Where did you hear that?"

"I overheard Lady Kingsley mention it as she and her son arrived. I am sure we'll hear the whole story at dinner."

"No doubt." She was tempted to plead a headache so she wouldn't have to witness her mother's reaction to Lord Caxton's presence at the party.

"Speaking of dinner, we shall be late if we don't hurry. Grace has pressed your emerald silk, which sets off your eyes so well. Kingsley can't help but be captivated." She rose, pulling Judith up with her, and bustled her out of the library and up to their rooms.

Judith couldn't help but wonder if Lord Caxton would be captivated as well.

\*\*\*\*

Judith hurried downstairs to the parlor a few minutes before her mother, who was busy lecturing Grace on the appropriate way to use a curling iron. Grace didn't usually serve as her mother's maid, but as Bates had been ill with a head cold, Lady Grangemore had insisted she stay in London.

Judith hoped to see Lord Caxton first so she would not need to fake surprise at the sight of him. Her mother's sharp eye was sure to notice, and she would be furious if she knew Judith had met him in the labyrinth and said nothing. Now if he'd cooperate and arrive a bit early as well…

Her breath caught when she noticed him standing at the window. The sea beyond was calm, wholly at odds with the waves frothing in her belly. Judith quickly scanned the room, but he was alone. She left the door open so as not to cause scandal and waited near the doorway, trying to calm her racing heart.

"Are you going to skulk there, Miss Leslie, or should I get you a glass of sherry?" he said without turning around.

She jumped. "I'm not skulking. And how did you know I was here?"

"Your perfume is distinctive. A unique mix of jasmine and roses."

"Is that the only reason?" she asked, a trifle breathlessly.

He turned then, his gaze smoldering. "No. I think

hereafter I shall always be able to sense when you have entered a room, whether I can smell you or not."

"Oh, my," she whispered. She was trapped in his gaze, as if it were drawing her closer to him. She took a step forward, pulled by an invisible string.

Voices in the hall broke the spell, halting her in her tracks. Peter smiled and went to the sideboard to pour her sherry, and she perched on the edge of a chair that was far more pretty than it was comfortable.

Lady Howley entered the room, followed by Judith's mother and another woman Judith did not know.

"Judith, there you are. Are you having sher…?" She broke off as Lord Caxton turned, two glasses in his hand. "You!"

Lord Caxton flashed a charming smile, although why he bothered Judith couldn't say. Her mother was entirely immune. "Good evening, Lady Grangemore, Lady Howley." He bowed to the other woman. "Your Grace."

"Caxton." She nodded her head regally.

Judith realized the woman must be Lady Kingsley, unless there were multiple duchesses in residence.

The duchess ran a calculating gaze up and down Peter's figure. "I heard you'd left London. Abandoning your bride already?"

"The bridegroom is superfluous at this stage, your Grace. I doubt my intended has even noticed I've gone."

Lady Kingsley let out a most un-regal snort. "Oh, she's noticed. And quite furious she is with you, too. I shouldn't be surprised if she cries off."

"That would be a tragedy of immeasurable

proportions."

Lady Kingsley emitted a bark Judith could only suppose was a laugh. "Upstart," she said, with a clear touch of amusement in her voice. She sat in a rather large armchair facing the window. "Pour me a sherry, and I won't tell your father where you are."

He bowed once again and handed her one of the glasses he'd already poured, then handed the other to Judith with a wink.

Judith's cheeks warmed, and she turned away, only to find herself at the receiving end of a glare from her mother.

"What brings you to Kent, Lord Caxton?" Lady Grangemore asked between clenched teeth as she perched in the chair which was the mate to Judith's. "I did not know you were acquainted with Lady Howley."

Lady Howley interjected. "I've known this handsome lad since he was a boy. Far more trouble than he's worth, then and now. I never imagined he'd accept my invitation once I heard he'd snagged himself a duke's daughter." She punched Caxton on the arm, causing him to spill the sherry he'd been about to hand to Lady Grangemore. A tall woman with a deep, raspy voice, Lady Howley was not known for her feminine poise and decorum. She was far more likely to be swilling brandy and smoking cigars with the men after dinner than sipping tea with the ladies. Judith rather liked her.

"As I told Lady Kingsley, my presence was not required in London, and it was high time I visited my godmother." He kissed her on the cheek, and she laughed.

"I didn't think you even remembered, godless

creature that you are."

Judith risked a glance at her mother. Judging from her fierce expression, she was not pleased to hear the man who'd been courting her daughter described in such a way.

"Now, now. I'm not godless, Aunt Gin. You'll give the ladies quite the wrong idea. And how could I ever forget you were my godmother? It's a never ending source of annoyance to my father." Caxton winked, resulting in a booming guffaw from his godmother and another snort from the duchess.

Judith barely refrained from laughing and failed utterly when she noticed her mother turning slightly green. She hid a giggle behind her hand, and then feeling guilty, changed the subject.

"Lady Howley, your house is magnificent. How long has it been in the family?"

"Thank you, my dear," Lady Howley said. "I would love to say it's been in the family for centuries, but my late husband won it in a card game in '98." Another guffaw. "We're very close to France here, you know, and the house's residents have a long history related to smuggling. 'Twas built by a lady pirate, over a hundred years ago, but the tunnels underneath are even older."

"A lady pirate, truly?" Judith asked, her interest piqued.

"Truly." Lady Howley grinned. "Jocasta, she was called. There's a portrait of her in the dining room you'll see at dinner. Uncommonly beautiful, with lovers in ports from here to the Indies." She paused, the better to hear the shocked gasps from Judith's mother.

Lady Howley smiled mischievously and continued.

"She retired here, possibly the wealthiest woman in the Kingdom, with one of her lovers. But one day she learned her man had been unfaithful. Discovering he planned to kill her and steal her money, she gathered all her riches and hid them in a chest, somewhere on the property." She paused. "Then she threw herself off the cliffs into the stormy sea."

"No!" Judith was fascinated. "What happened?"

"Her lover, Marcel, had planned to murder her that very night. He remained here after her death, slowly going mad hunting for the treasure. He wasted away and died in one of the tunnels. It was months before anyone found him, a miniature of Jocasta, torn in half, clutched in his skeletal hands."

"Oh, surely you're embellishing, Aunt Gin." Peter laughed, his tone smacking of incredulity.

"I am not. It's the God's honest truth." Lady Howley took a deep swallow of her sherry, and grinned.

"What a sad story!" Judith said. "Was the treasure ever found?"

"It remains hidden to this very day. Every square inch of this building has been searched since then. It's said that Marcel appears on the cliffs on nights when the moon is full and the sea is stormy, cursing Jocasta for foiling his plans."

A shiver marched up Judith's spine. Her mother appeared to be no less affected, her mouth slightly open, eyes wide. Judith flicked her gaze to Peter, who seemed far more interested in watching her than listening to the story. He winked again, the horrid man.

"But here comes the rest of our party at last," Lady Howley said. The room was invaded by seven more people, including Lord Kingsley. Although his mother would make an entertaining Dowager Duchess when he married, the duke himself was a nondescript sort of man, with wispy blond hair and an insipid expression. He seemed pleasant enough but Judith suspected his rank and money made him more attractive to women than his physical features.

Judith gave a polite curtsy to the remaining guests as they entered the room. Other than Peter, Lord Kingsley was the only eligible bachelor. The rest were debs like herself, and their mothers, all of whom fixed beady eyes on the gentlemen: Lady Ormonde and her daughter Rebecca, Lady St. George and her daughter Gwyneth, and Lady Wilcox trailed by her daughter Samantha. Judith was well acquainted with Gwyneth and quite happy to see her. She gave Gwyneth a quick embrace.

"Judith," Gwyneth said, "I had no idea you'd be here. I'm so glad to see a friendly, intelligent face." She cast a surreptitious glance over her shoulder at the other two girls. Rebecca was a dear, but her sweet disposition and her papa's fortune were her only assets. Samantha was so firmly under her manipulative mama's thumb that if she had ever possessed a personality, it was now thoroughly quashed.

Judith thanked providence none of Lady Cassandra's cronies were in attendance. They'd all be in London, preparing for…

Thoughts of the wedding pushed into her head, and she couldn't help turning to Lord Caxton. Would he go through with it? Would he marry her? The way he fixated on her, an expression of longing on his face, made her think he would not, although how he could extricate himself from the engagement without social disgrace she had no notion. And even if he did, how could Judith marry him?

"Judith." Her mother's sharp bark intruded on her thoughts just as she began to wonder when she'd started thinking of marriage to Peter Tenwick as a foregone conclusion if he were free.

"I'm so sorry," Judith said. "I was woolgathering."

Lady Wilcox nodded her head, a smirk upon her pinched face. "Comes from too much reading, I'm sure. We never taught Samantha to read. Very bad for girls. Gives them ideas, these novels."

Poor Samantha looked as if she'd like to melt into the floor. Judith couldn't possibly let such a ridiculous notion stand unchallenged, but before she could open her mouth her own mother spoke. "With all due respect, Lady Wilcox, I couldn't disagree more. Girls today are at a distinct disadvantage if they don't learn to read. How can a woman run a household if she hasn't a rudimentary knowledge of reading? Her servants would rob her blind, poor thing."

Judith almost cheered, feeling a rush of affection for her mother. She had never been treated any differently from her brothers in terms of education, at least not until they'd gone off to Eton. They'd had all the same lessons until then, from a governess, a music master, and a Classics tutor, and Judith had continued her studies alone after the boys had left. She spoke fluent French, passable Italian, and could read Latin and Greek. She devoured new novels as soon as she could acquire them.

She pitied Samantha. The written word had enriched her life immeasurably—she couldn't imagine what it would be like to leave such treasures undiscovered. Samantha, with red cheeks and watery eyes, ducked her head and studied her lap. Judith vowed to seek her out and teach her to read, if she could. She caught Gwyneth's eye and was sure her friend had the same idea.

Lady Howley broke the tension and changed the subject. "Come in, everyone, come in and sit down. Peter, dear, if you would be so kind as to pour the sherry? You've done so well at it." She winked, and Lord Caxton obliged, handing out glasses to all the ladies.

"I'll take a whisky, if you don't mind, Caxton," Lord Kingsley said, in a voice far deeper than his effeminate appearance would suggest. Judith couldn't help but wonder if it, and the preference for whisky, was cultivated to be at odds with his appearance.

"Of course," Lord Caxton said, the rich timbre of his voice perfectly suited to his own rugged and wholly masculine demeanor. Feeling unexpectedly warm, Judith took a swallow of her drink.

Her guests thus fortified, Lady Howley turned the talk to the weather and the latest fashions until they were called to dinner.

## Chapter 9

Going into dinner was not the staged affair it usually was at a party like this, as there were only two gentlemen present. Peter partnered Lady Kingsley, while the duke led Lady Howley. If Her Grace was insulted to be escorted by a mere viscount she certainly didn't show it, and when Peter switched the place cards to seat himself next to Judith, Lady Kingsley smirked in his direction.

He and Lord Kingsley pushed in the chairs of the ladies before taking their own seats around the long table. Set with elegantly simple white bone china and fine silver, delicate centerpieces of local wildflowers and driftwood had been placed at regular intervals along its length. Aunt Gin raised an eyebrow when Peter sat between Judith and Lady Gwyneth but said nothing. It was worth any censure to avoid sitting next to the odious Lady Wilcox, which is where he was supposed to be. Poor Kingsley's shoulders slumped when that woman, a predatory gleam in her eye, leaned in to engage him in conversation.

"Good evening, Miss Leslie," Peter said as the conversation began to hum around them.

"Lord Caxton."

"Your mother seems to want to rip my heart out with a fish fork."

Judith glanced at her mother on the other end of the

table, where she was fingering her fork, a malicious expression on her face. She turned back to him. "So she does. Should I allow her, do you think?"

"Could you stop her?"

Judith shrugged and dug into her first course, a cold soup. "I doubt it. She's not easily swayed once she's set her mind to something."

Peter frowned. "I am sorry to hear that. Do you share that trait?"

"No. I believe in giving people a chance to change my mind. It makes things more interesting, don't you agree?"

Relief flooded his chest. "I do! Oh, yes, I do. Wholeheartedly."

She stopped her spoon halfway to her mouth, her lips turned up at the corners. Oh, she was a sly one. Perhaps there was a way to convince her he was worth a second chance. Although if he didn't get out of this engagement, he might not be able to use it.

"Did you enjoy the pirate story Lady Howley related, Lord Caxton?" Judith had returned her spoon to her bowl and now glanced at the painting above the mantel, drawing Peter's eye. It was the painting their hostess had mentioned, of a stunning dark-haired woman in eighteenth century dress, a fortune in gold and jewels shining on her ears, fingers, and generous bosom. She had been beautiful, it was true, but she could not hold a candle to Judith.

"Peter," he said, returning his attention to the living. "You must call me Peter."

Judith frowned. "I think it's inappropriate to resume such familiarity, don't you?"

"We are friends, are we not?"

"That remains to be seen," she said with a sniff. "For now, you are Lord Caxton, and I haven't forgiven you."

Peter rubbed at the spot where, deep down, his heart ached at her statement. He let out a slow breath, but the pressure did not ease. He would change her mind; he had to.

He swallowed, adopted a light tone. "Very well. As to the pirate story, I've heard it many times. It is quite Aunt Gin's favorite. I think it's entirely rubbish, though. Surely there were no lady pirates."

"What? Oh, no. That's where you're wrong, my lord," she said, waving her spoon with such enthusiasm she spattered soup on his waistcoat. "Sorry." She put her spoon down and clasped her serviette, moving it toward him as if she were planning to wipe it herself. She stopped before she touched him and pulled her hand back. "Sorry," she repeated, and handed him the napkin.

Peter blotted the spot, and a footman appeared magically at his side. He took the soiled napkin and handed a fresh one to Judith.

"You were saying?" Peter asked.

"I was saying that of course there are female pirates. Have you never heard of Anne Bonny, or Mary Read?"

"Pray, enlighten me."

"There is a book in the library; I noticed it this morning. I've already read it, as we have it at home. You should read it—perhaps you'll learn something."

His cat had apparently sharpened her claws. "How intriguing. Surely it is a fictional account."

"It is not. It's a history of pirates. *Women* pirates."

She knit her brows together, clearly exasperated. "You men are all the same, aren't you? Entirely too convinced of your own superiority to believe a woman could do the same things a man can do."

"Do you see, Lady Grangemore? This is what becomes of teaching a girl to read." Lady Wilcox's strident tones intruded on Judith's defense of women. The woman had trained her beady eyes on Lady Grangemore but was pointing at Judith. "Discussing piracy at the dinner table, and asserting that women are equal to men?" She shook her head in disgust. Judith's mouth dropped open in surprise, and her mother sprang to her defense once again.

"I have never taught my daughter she is inferior to men, nor does our family treat her as such. You may find it important to teach your daughter she is unworthy, but I never will."

Peter was tempted to applaud, and by the twitching of Judith's hands, he suspected she was feeling the same way. Lady Wilcox, however was not. She sputtered and glared at the assembled company, then pushed her chair away from the table.

"I am sorry, Lady Howley, but suddenly I find myself quite unwell. I believe I shall retire. Come, Samantha."

"But, I'm…" Samantha attempted to protest, but a glare from her mother quelled any thought of rebellion. She set down her spoon and sighed audibly. "Yes, Mother." She had a tiny voice, as if there wasn't enough life inside her to make more sound. But as she followed her mother out of the room, she turned and flashed a brilliant smile at Judith.

"Poor Samantha," Lady Gwyneth whispered in his

left ear. "I do hope she is freed one day and marries a man who will let her speak her mind."

Peter turned to face her. "Do you think she will?"

"Judith and I shall help her, assuming Lady Wilcox lets her out of her sight. Won't we, Judith?"

He turned back to Judith, who was blotting her lips with her napkin.

"Yes, we will," she said. Further conversation was stalled as the footmen brought in the fish course, and Peter was left contemplating this woman who became more fascinating every time she opened her mouth.

****

Judith fully expected a lecture from her mother after the incident with Lady Wilcox, but it never came. Her mother squeezed her arm as they left the dining room. The two gentlemen decided not to partake of brandy and cigars and instead followed the ladies into the drawing room directly after dinner. Realizing she was safe from reprimand, at least for that, she relaxed into her chair.

Until Lord Caxton sat beside her. When he gazed at her, it was as if the air left the room, and every muscle in her body tensed. She pasted a smile on her face.

"You look bilious, Miss Leslie."

The breath whooshed from her lungs in a half snort, half laugh that earned her a glare from her mother.

So much for the reprieve.

"You are the soul of charm, Lord Caxton," Judith said.

"I am simply honest. You *did* look a bit bilious, but now when you smile, you are stunning."

She laughed again, this time without the snort. "Charming indeed. You could quite turn a girl's head."

"Have I?" His eyes twinkled, the corners of his lips turned up.

He was smiling at her again, and her brain went fuzzy. "I'm sorry. Have you what?"

"Turned your head."

She was silent for a moment. Had he? Certainly, before he'd gotten engaged to another woman. Now she couldn't afford to let him get close again. It would not end well.

"No." She rose and walked to the other side of the room, where Gwyneth was deliberately not engaged in conversation with Rebecca. If anyone looked bilious, it was Rebecca.

"Care for a turn about the room, Gwyneth?"

Gwyneth peeked over Judith's shoulder, presumably at Lord Caxton. Judith did not turn around; she had no wish to see what he was doing. "Certainly." She rose and looped her arm around Judith's.

"What is going on between you and the handsome Lord Caxton?" Gwyneth asked as they made their first circuit around the room.

"Nothing at all, of course. He's engaged to another."

"So I hear. Why is he here, then, and not in London?"

"He claims he's here to visit his godmother."

"Hmm," Gwyneth said. "That must be why he chose to sit next to you on the opposite side of the room, and why his eyes are tracking your every movement."

"Don't be ridiculous," Judith said, but she could

feel his gaze. It warmed her from within, a cup of chocolate on a cold morning. She shook her head.

Her friend smirked. "I knew it. You are in love with him."

Love? Was she? No. Not love. "I admire him, it's true, and rather like him. But love seems a bit premature." No, not love, although the butterflies battling in her stomach might have disagreed.

Judith risked a glance at Lord Caxton, now engaged in conversation with Samantha, who had been allowed to rejoin the company after dinner. The poor girl looked rather thunderstruck. Whatever else he may be, there was no denying Lord Caxton was a dynamic presence. Perhaps feeling her regard, he grinned at Judith.

Judith stumbled. Lord Caxton chuckled and turned his attention back to Samantha.

"Whatever is wrong with you?" Gwyneth asked. "I've been talking for five minutes and you haven't so much as nodded, and now you're tripping over imaginary rocks in the drawing room."

"I did not trip over anything but my hem," Judith lied. "And I was listening."

"No, you weren't. When I realized you weren't attending, I rattled off a string of nonsense, and you didn't bat an eye."

Judith blushed. "Fine, I wasn't listening. I was thinking."

"About Lord Caxton, I assume."

It pained her to admit it, but she did. "Yes. But the man is engaged to another." Her stomach clenched as she thought of Cassandra. That she should be the one to claim him was upsetting in the extreme.

"True. But as I said before, the fact he's here with you and not in London with her is telling, don't you think?"

"He likes to do the unexpected. It doesn't mean he won't go through with the wedding. The scandal would be devastating for Cassandra, and even he would not defy convention in such a manner. It does not do to make enemies with a duke, especially one as powerful as Bothwell."

And that realization made her sad. He was, at heart, a kind man, and he would not treat a woman in such a way, even if he had no part in arranging the match, even if he had made an occupation of defying his father.

She sighed deeply, blinked away a tear. "If you don't mind, Gwyneth, I believe I'll retire. I'm feeling a bit tired."

Gwyneth's eyes were sympathetic as she embraced Judith, her expression nearly undoing the composure Judith was trying so hard to maintain. She bit down on her bottom lip, eased out a slow breath.

"Good night, Gwyneth. If you would please tell my mother I've gone up?"

"Of course. Good night, Judith. Do sleep well, and try not to dwell on things you cannot change."

\*\*\*\*

Poor Samantha having been dragged away by her mother, again, Peter was at leisure to study the two women as they turned about the room and smiled whenever he caught Judith glancing at him. Then just as abruptly as she joined her friend in their walk, she fled as if her skirts were aflame.

With difficulty he controlled his impulse to follow

her. Her friend watched her go, then turned and sat next to him.

"Good evening, Lord Caxton."

"Lady Gwyneth, yes?"

"Yes." She was nearly as tall as he was, at least when they were sitting. She met his eyes, her expression deadly serious. "What are you doing here, Lord Caxton?"

He nearly squirmed under her regard. "I am visiting my godmother."

"You haven't seen Lady Howley in several years, or so I understand. Why now?"

"Why not?"

"It wouldn't have anything to do with the fact Miss Leslie was here?"

Peter shrugged. It was the only way to avoid admitting the truth of her statement.

"I thought so." Lady Gwyneth nodded. "You should leave, my lord. You'll never extricate yourself from your engagement to Lady Cassandra, and your being here is confusing—and hurting—Judith."

"I could never cause her pain, Lady Gwyneth."

"So you say, but I understand you've already done it once, and now here you are, and she's run off to cry alone in her room."

"What?" Judith didn't seem the sort to cry over anything. She was far too strong. He half rose to go after her when he felt a firm tug on his arm.

"Sit down, Lord Caxton. You can't very well go to her room. Just be gone by morning." She gave him a look that brooked no argument, then rose to join her mother on the other side of the room.

Peter leaned back in his chair. Lady Gwyneth had a

point, much as it pained him to admit it.

What *was* he doing here?

He should be attempting to get out of his engagement, not tormenting poor Judith. But not being with her was not possible. She filled his senses. Her jasmine rose scent lingered in the air, or so he imagined. His fingers itched to touch her luscious auburn hair. He could still feel the way she fit next to him when they danced, and his lips still tingled from their last kiss.

No, it was not possible to be away from her. He would find a new suitor for Cassandra, and he would win Judith's heart. Living without her simply was not an option.

## Chapter 10

After a sleepless night tossing and turning and trying not to think about Peter Tenwick, Judith went down early to breakfast. Perhaps a walk in the sea air would clear her head of thoughts of him.

And perhaps it would have, were the man himself not already in the dining room.

She stopped and turned on her heel to leave, hoping he hadn't seen her.

"Miss Leslie."

Bloody hell. She pivoted to face him. "Lord Caxton."

"Leaving so soon?"

God, he was handsome. His dark blond hair was uncombed, giving him an adorably mussed look. His waistcoat was a glossy teal today, a color that complemented his blue eyes, which were twinkling with amusement at her discomfiture.

"I, uh, forgot something."

"Your reticule?"

"Um, yes," she said, before realizing it was in her hand. "I mean, no." She tossed the bag on the table and sat opposite him. "Oh, never mind. I was leaving because I didn't want to talk to you."

His eyes lost their sparkle and he seemed genuinely pained. "Why not?"

"Because this…" she wiggled her fingers at him,

"this whatever it is can go nowhere. You are engaged, and you should stop flirting with me and go home."

"I don't want to go home," he said, his tone husky.

Judith said nothing, just rose to fill a plate with food from the sideboard. She did so automatically, but her appetite was gone.

She felt him behind her, closed her eyes. His body warmed hers, even without touch. She bit back a moan as he leaned toward her, his breath at her ear.

"I want to stay here, with you. Even if it's the last thing I should be doing."

She opened her mouth to tell him to stop, but the words wouldn't come. She didn't want him to stop.

He traced her earlobe with a finger. "You have perfect ears; did you know that? Nibblesome." His lips replaced his finger, and he trailed kisses down the side of her neck.

She leaned back instinctively, tilted her head to the side. Sensation from his touch shot down her spine, pooling at the base, spreading from her back around her hips to the private spot between her legs.

Then suddenly he was gone, and Judith was aware of a throat being cleared somewhere in the room. She nearly dropped her plate as she turned around, her face hot, her groin tingling.

Gwyneth stood there, her mouth set into a grim line.

Judith risked a glance at Peter, who winked. She couldn't stop a grin but masked it quickly and returned to her seat. "Good morning, Gwyneth. I hope you're well."

"Not as well as you are, apparently." She filled her own plate then sat next to Judith. "What a surprise to see you here, Lord Caxton. Didn't you say you were leaving this morning?"

Judith's gaze flicked between the two. She was missing something.

"I can't imagine where you got that idea, Lady Gwyneth," Peter said, then shoveled a forkful of eggs into his mouth.

Gwyneth speared a sausage with unusual malice.

Judith cocked her head at Peter. "What is going on here?" Peter arched his forehead and shrugged, the picture of innocence.

Gwyneth glared at him. "My mistake, it seems," she said.

"So, what are you ladies planning to do this morning?" Peter asked, in a deft move to prevent Gwyneth from stabbing him with her fork. "It promises to be a beautiful day."

Grateful for the change in subject, Judith said, "I was planning a walk after breakfast. And I understand Lady Howley has arranged an excursion to the beach this afternoon."

"Capital. May I join you on your walk?"

"No, you may not," Gwyneth said primly. "I have some matters I wish to discuss with Judith."

"You do?" Judith asked.

"Yes," Gwyneth said, "don't you remember?" She gave Judith a pointed look.

"Oh. Yes, of course, I do." Judith said, more confused. "I am sorry, Lord Caxton. Perhaps we will see you on the beach." She pushed her untouched plate away and stood. "I'll get my wrap, Gwyneth. Shall I meet you in the front hall?"

"I'm coming." Gwyneth rose as well and took

Judith's arm. "Shall we?"

Judith allowed herself to be propelled out of the room and out the front door. "My wrap?"

"You don't need one. It's quite warm."

It was indeed warm, but the sun was in her eyes and she missed her bonnet. Gwyneth was clearly not to be deterred, however, and they were halfway through the garden before Judith dug in her heels.

"What has gotten into you, Gwyneth?"

Gwyneth toyed with a curl at her ear, a sure sign she didn't want to talk about something.

"Well?" Judith resisted the impulse to stomp her foot.

Gwyneth sighed. "Fine. Last night after you retired, I advised Lord Caxton to return to London."

"What? Why on earth would you do that?"

"Because he's not good for you, Judith. He can't marry you, of course, and I don't want to see you ruined by him."

Judith tamped down her rising fury. She took a deep breath. "I appreciate your trying to protect me, Gwyneth."

"But you'd like me to mind my own business."

"Yes."

Gwyneth grasped Judith by the shoulders. "I can't. Not after what I saw in the dining room."

Judith's flesh heated as she remembered Peter's touch, his kisses on her neck, the sweet smell of tea of his breath. "Nothing happened," she lied.

"Please, Judith. I'm not a fool. I saw very well what happened and can easily imagine what *might* have happened had I not walked in when I did. You're lucky it was me and not Lady Wilcox."

Gwyneth regarded her with a pleading expression. "Promise me you will keep your distance from him, Judith. Please? I will have no choice but to tell your mother if you don't."

"You'll tell my mother what, exactly?"

"That you are becoming dangerously close to Lord Caxton, a confirmed rogue who is engaged to another woman."

Every instinct told Judith her friend was right. Just as her heart told her she couldn't stay away from the man. For now, she hugged Gwyneth. "I promise," she whispered, knowing she'd break it in a heartbeat if given the opportunity.

\*\*\*\*

The day remained as fine as Lord Caxton had promised. The sky was a vivid blue with only a wispy cloud here and there. Now attired in her bonnet and a wrap, Judith still blinked at the bright sun as they made their way to the open carriages that would take them to the beach.

Judith and her mother rode with Lady Howley, Gwyneth, and her mother. Judith suspected Gwyneth had somehow arranged this so she could keep an eye on her.

"Don't be dismayed at the sight of the buildings in town. Folkestone has decayed somewhat in recent years, but the natural landscape is as beautiful as ever. Rumor has it they are making plans to build a railway with a stop here. We are close to France, after all. On a day such as this one, you can see all the way to the French coast." Lady Howley continued in this vein, pointing out interesting sites and landmarks for the edification of her visitors. After a while Judith stopped listening, as the views of the sea were far more interesting than their hostess' lecture. The dark blue waters of the Channel sparkled in the sun, contrasting with the bright greens and browns of the rocky landscape they passed. The waves lapped gently on the beach beneath them, punctuated by the occasional cries of a seabird.

Turning her attention away from the water, Judith kept her gaze fixed on the back of Peter's head as he rode in the other carriage, his hair ruffling in the breeze. He was leaning toward Lord Kingsley, engaged in animated conversation, gesturing wildly with his hands.

Gorgeous hands, strong, with long fingers. Hands that could be gentle, bringing pleasure and delicious sensation. But now they were simply tools for emphasis, never still. He pointed this way and that, and at one point he nearly knocked Lady Ormonde's magnificent hat off her head.

"What is so amusing?" Gwyneth whispered in her ear.

Judith blinked. "Amusing?"

"You laughed out loud."

"Did I?" She'd had no idea. It *had* been funny to see Lady Ormonde smack the top of her hat to press it more securely onto her head, then glare at a clearly oblivious Peter. She wanted to know what he was talking about.

Her response did not please her friend. "Yes, you did. It was Lord Caxton, I assume, who caught your attention."

"Actually, it was Lady Ormonde. Didn't you see her almost lose her hat? What *is* that on the brim, can you tell? It looks like a drunken possum."

Mollified, Gwyneth giggled, earning them both frowns from their respective mothers. Undeterred from her mission, Lady Howley acted as if nothing untoward had occurred, and continued her dissertation on the bird life of Kent.

Thus diverted from her perusal of the back of Lord Caxton's strong hands and handsome head, Judith spent the rest of the ride in whispered conversation with Gwyneth about nothing in particular. She was almost disappointed when they arrived at their destination, which proved to be a derelict pier jutting into the water from a sandy beach. The tide was out, so there was plenty of room to explore. It was a bit chilly for swimming despite the warmth of the day, so Judith was pleased not to have to change into a bathing costume.

Lady Howley, however, had no such qualms. After inviting other women to join her but hearing only refusal, she strode to a lone bathing machine not far from the pier and disappeared inside. The footman who accompanied them to the beach pushed it into the water then discreetly withdrew. Although fascinated to see what the eccentric woman might put on, Judith allowed herself to be led off by Gwyneth to explore the pools left by the receding tide.

After a short while, Gwyneth was called away by her mother, so Judith stood alone by the shore, poking at a crab with a piece of driftwood when a cloud obscured the sun.

"What are you doing to that poor crustacean?" the cloud asked in a familiar voice.

Judith shaded her eyes with a hand and peered at Lord Caxton. She leaned back on her heels. "Goodness. You are large, aren't you?"

"There's the refreshing candor you exhibited on the night we met," he said, laughing. "I wondered when I might see it again."

"I'm not sure my mother would call it either refreshing or candid. She's much more apt to call it impulsive and obnoxious."

"How fortunate she's over there, then." He waved his hand in the general direction of the pier.

Judith scanned the beach for the rest of the guests. Lady Howley's white head floated in the water, and the others roamed on various parts of the beach in groups of two, three, and four, leaving Judith quite alone with Peter. She was sure neither her mother nor Gwyneth would approve.

Excitement surged through her veins.

"Shall we explore those caves, Lord Caxton?" She pointed to a dark patch at the end of the beach.

"I doubt we'll get there before your mother stops us, but I'm willing if you are." He winked, and the thrill settled into her belly, where it completely overran her good sense.

She looped her arm through his, and they set off down the beach.

"You seem quite at home near the water, Miss Leslie, yet I believe you come from the Midlands, do you not?"

"I do. But my mother is Scottish, and we spent our summers on Loch Lomond. I swim like a fish."

"How intriguing." His gaze roamed the length of her body as if he were gauging her buoyancy. "What sort of fish?"

"Does it matter?"

"Certainly. Fish are quite different, you know.

There are those which swim near the surface, stopping now and then to snatch a dragonfly. Others stay near the bottom, flitting over the sand and feeding off scraps other creatures leave behind, drab in color and usually quite ugly. Then there are fish who swim near the middle, neither too cold nor too warm, too dark nor too light. Those fish, of course, are the most vibrant and colorful." He stopped and looked her over once again. "Yes, I believe you'd be that sort of fish. Beautiful, swift, and clever, gracefully dancing in the rays of the sun filtering through the water."

Judith's mouth dropped open. Never had anyone called her beautiful, let alone graceful.

"I've rendered you speechless. Is that a first?"

Judith snapped her mouth shut. "Yes, I rather think it is. What a lovely thing to say. I'm sure no one has ever used any of those words to describe me, let alone all of them in a single sentence."

He reached out and stroked her cheek. "They are all true."

Judith swallowed hard, her mouth suddenly dry. "Oh, my," she said, her voice croaky. She stared at his lips, willing him to kiss her even as one part of her brain knew they'd be spotted.

He licked his lips but kept his distance, dropped his hand to his side. "I believe we have caves to explore, Miss Leslie. Shall we?"

Before they had walked four steps down the beach, a shrill voice called her name. Judith stopped and sighed. "That's Mama. I fear our adventures today are at an end, Lord Caxton."

They turned to see Lady Grangemore advancing toward them at a pace that was surprisingly rapid, given the terrain and her voluminous skirts. Judith knew then her mother had seen Lord Caxton touch her face. If she wasn't in a carriage bound for Derbyshire by the end of the day, she'd be very shocked indeed.

"Judith! What are you doing?" Lady Grangemore was upon them, her expression fierce.

"We were simply walking, like everyone else," Judith said.

"Everyone else has finished walking and returned to the carriages. Did you not see the storm clouds?"

Sure enough, an enormous bank of dark clouds loomed just offshore, moving swiftly inland. She glanced worriedly at Peter, who was regarding the clouds with obvious alarm.

"Come, both of you," Lady Grangemore said. "We are in grave danger of a soaking if we don't hurry." She grabbed Judith's hand and dragged her away, Lord Caxton on their heels.

They were only a few yards from the carriages, no longer open to the elements, when the heavens opened. Rain fell in a torrent, as if someone had upended a bathtub over their heads.

They broke into a run, or as close to a run as they could get in their gowns. Judith shrieked as her feet left the ground, and she found herself in Lord Caxton's arms. He grinned at her as he raced them to the vehicles and all but tossed her into one. He went back to assist Judith's mother, grasping her at the waist, depositing her in the carriage, and disappearing.

It all happened so fast Judith had barely drawn breath before the vehicle began to move. Rain rapped on the roof of the carriage, almost deafening the occupants. Water dripped from her hat onto her lap.

Her mother cleared her throat, returning Judith's attention to the inside. Beside her, Gwyneth grinned, but in the opposite seat Lady St. George wore a pinched expression as she regarded Judith. Lady Grangemore's fierce scowl was at odds with her bedraggled appearance, her skirts sodden and the feathers on her hat flattened against her cheek. Judith bit her lip to keep from laughing—that would not go over well at all.

"*What* were you thinking, young lady?" her mother said between clenched teeth.

"We were simply walking, Mama, and didn't notice the storm."

"I saw him touch your face. That was no mere walk, Judith."

"He was wiping a bit of sand off my cheek, Mama. It was nothing." Judith hoped she was lying better than she usually did.

"It certainly appeared intimate from where I was," Gwyneth said.

Judith glared at her friend. "You're not helping," she whispered.

"I don't intend to help you, Judith," Gwyneth whispered back. "This is dangerous ground you're treading upon."

Judith ignored her, returning her attention to the rain. Observing the others with one eye, she waited for her mother to pounce again. A flash of lightning caused everyone to jump, then jump again when it was followed by a deafening crack of thunder. Wind whipped water into the carriage, soaking everyone's skirts.

"Where is Lady Howley?" Lady Grangemore asked, in an obvious attempt to keep them from dwelling on certain death from drowning.

"She's in the other carriage. She wanted to give the other guests the same recitation she gave to us on the way here."

"I shouldn't think there would be sufficient room. Or that anyone could hear her through this storm," Lady Grangemore yelled, another clap of thunder all but drowning her out.

"I understand Lord Kingsley returned to the house on foot before the storm broke," Lady St. George said.

"How odd. It must be five miles. He'll be soaked through."

Lady St. George shrugged. She was not interested in the Duke of Kingsley, which wasn't a surprise. From the age of three, Gwyneth had been promised to an earl who held the neighboring estate. Her first London season was only a formality. Judith was rather jealous, truth be told. Gwyneth and Roger had grown up together and were the best of friends. It was a strategic as well as a love match, and she couldn't imagine anything as perfect as that.

If she tried, she could still feel Lord Caxton's strong arms around her body, the smell of his musky cologne as he touched her cheek. She sighed, brushed a wet strand of hair off her face, and watched the rain.

## Chapter 11

In the parlor before dinner, Lady Howley's guests were talking about nothing but being caught in the storm. The rain continued to pelt the windows, punctuated by great claps of thunder that seemed to the shake the very foundations of the house. Samantha and Rebecca giggled and whispered behind their fans every time they spotted Peter or Judith.

Although Judith steadfastly avoided him—perhaps in a futile attempt to curtail the gossip—it was apparent their walk had not gone unnoticed. Even as his fingers itched to touch her again, to do so would ruin her.

After Peter returned to the house, wetter than he he'd ever been, his valet had helped him to bathe and dress in dry clothing. He had sat in front of the fire sipping a brandy as he contemplated his situation. Lady Cassandra had clearly reveled in playing the outraged fiancée, judging by Lady Kingsley's comments when he'd arrived. Even though the duchess had promised not to tell his father where he'd gone, it was not beyond the realm of possibility one of the other ladies had written to friends in London, mentioning his presence at the house party. Gossip spread through the *ton* faster than the plague, so his whereabouts were unlikely to be a secret to his father, or his fiancée, for long.

Now he stood at the mantel, watching Judith talking to Lady Gwyneth. He had been fanciful, with his talk of colorful fish, but she had responded in a surprising way. He found it hard to believe no one had ever called her beautiful, unless perhaps they had used the word 'stunning' instead. She was less like a fish than a magnificent horse, however, with her chestnut mane and long legs. He could imagine them beneath her gown, smooth and muscled…

He shook his head before he wound up with an erection that would be hard to hide. He turned from the sight of Judith as Lord Kingsley approached him. The man was at least a head shorter than Peter. A pleasant enough chap, but his lip was adorned with a wispy mustache so resembling custard Peter always felt the impulse to hand him a handkerchief so he could wipe it off.

"Kingsley," he said, nodding his head in greeting.

"Caxton. I understand congratulations are in order."

"So I'm told."

Kingsley raised a blond brow to match his mustache. "It's a good match. You're not pleased?"

"Not particularly. Lady Cassandra and I have little in common, and we don't know each other at all. I suspect she has no more interest in marrying me than I have in her." He took a sip of his drink and regarded Kingsley over the rim of his glass. "She'd throw me over in an instant if a suitable noble of higher rank offered for her."

Kingsley appeared thoughtful. Peter had planted the seed. "She *is* beautiful," the duke said. "And comes from a well-respected family."

Peter's gaze wandered to Judith, who was laughing. God, she was even gorgeous when she laughed.

Kingsley cleared his throat. "Oh, I see."

Peter returned his attention to his companion. "You see what, exactly?"

"I see what has caused your lack of enthusiasm for the match with Lady Cassandra. Miss Leslie is a striking woman, with a lively intellect. She'd make a suitable bride for someone of your rank."

Peter was surprised by the depth of emotion the duke's words stirred within him. Kingsley seemed to have as little regard for women as Peter's father, considering them little more than chattel.

Compelled to come to Judith's defense, he said, "She'd make a suitable bride for anyone, regardless of rank. You should be so lucky as to attract her attention, Kingsley. Now if you'll excuse me?" He strode away before the duke could reply and joined Judith and Lady Gwyneth on the settee.

"Good evening, ladies. How did you enjoy our little sojourn on the beach?"

"My sojourn was not nearly as exciting as yours, I think, Lord Caxton," Lady Gwyneth said with a pinched expression. "And I was quite dry, at least until Judith joined us in the carriage."

"You can hardly blame me for that, Gwyn. The rain was slanting sideways."

"It was rather exhilarating, don't you think, Miss Leslie? Racing the storm?" Peter said. He was gratified to see her blush to the roots of her hair, presumably remembering how he'd carried her in his arms for the last part of that race. He ached to have her there again, in private and out of the rain.

"I understand Lady Howley plans to take us down

to the secret passages under the house tomorrow, since it's expected to rain again," Judith said.

Gwyneth frowned. "I have no interest in traipsing around in dark musty caverns. Surely you're not planning to go, Judith?"

"I am, actually. This house has quite an intriguing history, and I would love to hear more. Don't you remember the hidden treasure story Lady Howley related on our first night? How exciting it would be to find it!" Her green eyes flashed.

"I very much doubt there's any treasure. What do you think, Lord Caxton?" Gwyneth asked.

"Miss Leslie and I are of like mind. I would love to hunt for treasure. It would certainly make for a more interesting diversion than one finds at most country house parties."

He glanced at Judith, who was smiling at him. He vowed to have her smile like that at him at every possible opportunity.

****

The rain continued throughout the night and the morning of the next day. After listening to Rebecca sing off-key at an impromptu morning recital, Samantha accompanying on the pianoforte (if one could call it accompaniment), Judith and her ears were eager to go exploring. Once luncheon was finished and her mother retired for a nap, Judith donned a sturdy pair of boots and the drabbest gown she had.

They met in the drawing room. Judith was a bit surprised to see only Lady Howley, Lord Kingsley, and Lord Caxton. She had expected at least one of the other ladies to join them. Where was their spirit of adventure?

"I'm so delighted you wish to join us, Miss Leslie,"

Lady Howley said. She was wearing what looked suspiciously like a pair of pantaloons. Her gaze traveled from Judith's faded olive green muslin to her worn brown leather boots. "And dressed so sensibly, I see. Although you would do much better in these." She modeled her garment, which was indeed a pair of pantaloons in a gray silk. A matching blouse was tucked into them, with a black leather belt around her waist.

Judith fingered her skirt, rather jealous.

"You will get dirty, I'm afraid," Lady Howley continued. "Are you sure you wish to wear those trousers, Kingsley? They seem very fine."

He shrugged. "These old things?"

Peter rolled his eyes at Judith, and Lady Howley directed them out the door toward the kitchen. The staff were busy clearing up after luncheon; no one paid any notice when their mistress sauntered past them wearing trousers, a line of aristocrats trailing behind her like baby ducks.

They stopped at a wooden door at the end of a corridor, a huge round, metal handle proclaiming its age. "This is the oldest part of the house, built in the fourteenth century. Our lady pirate tore down the original and built on top of these tunnels. The steps are quite uneven and the ceiling rather low, so do be careful." She peered up at Peter, at least a head taller than herself. "Especially you, Peter dear. I should be annoyed if you knock yourself unconscious and we have to drag you back up the steps."

"Duly noted, milady," Peter said with a laugh.

Lady Howley opened the door with a creak; a rush of cool, dank air escaped, smelling of fish, mildew, and adventure.

"How often do you venture down here, Lady Howley?" Judith asked.

"We keep the hinges oiled and the steps clear. You never know when you might need an escape route." She winked, then leaned over a basket Judith hadn't noticed by the door. Lady Howley pulled out four torches, lit them from the sconce on the wall, and handed them around. "You'll need these. It's quite dark."

Trepidation and excitement warred in Judith's belly, but she followed Lady Howley down the stone steps, Peter directly behind her. His presence at her back was comforting. Lady Howley had not lied about the condition of the steps. Centuries of use had worn them down in uneven patterns. She could imagine the pirate queen running down them for an assignation with her lover. She stumbled slightly and felt a steadying hand on her shoulder.

The staircase began to twist and turn until Judith had no idea what direction she faced. Finally, they reached the end and stepped into a cavernous room cut from stone. Lady Howley lit several wall sconces with her torch, and the room filled with flickering light. Judith jumped at a noise from the shadows near the floor.

Lady Howley chuckled. "It's only a rat, my dear. I'm afraid these caverns are full of them."

"What is this room?" Kingsley asked, his voice unusually small and his face slightly off-color.

"I believe it was a store room for smuggled goods, judging by the kegs and crockery we found along the wall when we first purchased the house. There are even a few kegs left." She aimed her torch at the corner, revealing a pile of wooden barrels with rusty metal bands.

Judith drew her finger in the dust that covered them. "What's inside?"

"Wine, most likely. It traveled better in kegs than in bottles. It might be rum, however, depending on where it originated."

"You never looked inside? Perhaps that's where the treasure is hidden!"

"They're only about forty years old," Lady Howley said, "long after the treasure was hidden. No, the treasure, if it exists, is somewhere else. Let's keep walking, shall we? There's another room I want to show you."

She led them out of the store room down another set of labyrinthine corridors, lighting an occasional sconce on the way. Judith was sure without those they'd never find their way back to the house.

After what seemed like miles of walking in the damp darkness, Judith spied a light ahead, and the smell of the sea grew stronger. The corridor opened into another large room, this one more brightly lit from a man-sized hole in the wall. She walked toward it, only to have Peter hold out a hand, blocking her way.

"Careful, Miss Leslie. If I'm not mistaken, that is an opening in the cliffside."

Judith bristled at the caution. "I'm not going to jump off the edge, Lord Caxton." She pushed past him and stood with her toes near the edge. The rain had stopped, and the sea lay before her, about fifty feet down. At the base of the cliff, water lapped gently against weathered rocks. The air smelled fresh, wet, pure, as if the world had been cleansed. She inhaled deeply, letting it wash over her. A mild wind whistled around her head, loosening her hair from its pins.

Lady Howley joined her. "I love the smell too. Nothing like it." She nodded approvingly, as if Judith had passed a test of some kind. "When the tide is out, there are lovely pools at the base of these cliffs, beneath the cave. You can often see seals sunning themselves on the rocks."

"Surely this isn't the only opening to these caves. How would smugglers get their goods inside?" Judith asked.

"There is another opening farther down, on the beach. You can see grooves in the rock from centuries of heavily laden carts rolling into the cave."

"I'd like to see that. Wouldn't you, Lord Caxton?" Judith asked.

"Certainly." He stood behind her, his presence solid and comforting.

A moan from beside Judith drew their attention. Lord Kingsley had grown distinctly green in hue, and he sank to the floor in a dead faint.

"Kingsley?" Lady Howley rushed to him. She pulled a fan out of a pocket in her pantaloons and waved it at him. His eyelids flickered open and he moaned again. "Whatever is the matter with you?"

"Heights. Closed spaces. Can't stand them."

Lady Howley rolled her eyes. "Then why on earth did you come with us, ridiculous man?"

"To be fair, Aunt Gin, one doesn't expect heights in cellars under one's house," Peter said reasonably.

Lady Howley ignored him. She pulled a flask from another pocket—really, what else did she have in there?—and held it to his lips. "Drink a bit of brandy, and then we'll go back to the house."

"Oh, no," Judith said. "Do we have to?" She was immediately contrite. Of course they did. Kingsley was obviously unwell, and she couldn't very well stay in the caverns on her own.

Lady Howley's gaze flicked from her to Peter, a mischievous glint in her eye. "Peter, perhaps you can escort Judith to the other cave entrance? It's easy to find—you turn right when you go out into the corridor and the path curves down until you reach it. You can't possibly get lost. Follow the lit sconces back to the house."

"Oh, no," Judith said. "It wouldn't be proper. My mother would kill me if she found out."

"She'll never know," Lady Howley said. "You'll be back before she wakes from her afternoon nap, and Peter will be every inch the gentleman, won't you, dear?"

Peter put his hand to his heart. "Absolutely." He turned to Judith. "What do you say, Miss Leslie? Shall we continue our adventure?"

She moved her mouth to say no, they mustn't, but "Yes, let's" came out instead. Before she knew it, Peter had placed her hand in his, and they headed deeper into the cave.

## Chapter 12

Peter exchanged a glance with his godmother as they left. Placing a hand on his arm, she said, "Don't get lost, now." And winked.

Was she telling him he *should* get lost? Perhaps she didn't want him to marry Lady Cassandra either. Getting lost alone in the caves with Judith would ensure he'd have to marry her, whether he found a replacement suitor for Cassandra or not. But would she want to, or would she be like his own mother, forced to marry a man she didn't love because of one indiscretion?

"Would you rather go back to the house, Lord Caxton?" He hadn't realized he'd stopped. She was gazing up at him with those deep green eyes, and all thoughts of propriety flew out of his head.

"No. I'd much rather be here with you. Unless, of course, you're having second thoughts."

She smiled at him. "No."

"Very well. Let's proceed." He still held her hand in his, gently squeezed. It was smooth, soft, and she was tall enough that he didn't need to reach down to hold it. He remembered their last kiss, remembered how they'd fit together like two pieces of a puzzle. He wanted to kiss her again but had promised his godmother he would be a gentleman.

Gentlemanly behavior was highly overrated.

He turned her to face him, stroked her cheek with

his other hand. Her lips parted, and she drew in a sharp, expectant breath.

He couldn't resist.

He leaned down and pressed his lips to hers. She tasted of apples from the tart they'd had for dessert. Sweet, spicy with cinnamon. He did love apple tarts.

His tongue explored her lips, gently pushed to enter her mouth. She moaned and pressed against him, and he found again that they fit perfectly. He cupped the back of her head with one hand, placed the other at the small of her back. Even through layers of clothing he could feel her heart race under his palm. His tongue went deeper, dancing with her own. His cock strained against his trousers, but he ignored it—stealing a kiss was one thing, but anything more would be quite another.

He pulled away from her with difficulty, cupped her cheek in his hand. Tendrils of auburn hair hugged her cheeks, making her look deliciously tousled. "You are so beautiful, Judith. I could kiss you the rest of my days and never weary of it."

She licked her lips again and leaned back against the cool stone wall. "I wish that were an option for us, my lord." She let out a long breath, her expression rather sad.

"I will make it happen, if you'll have me."

Her eyes widened. "But how?"

"Have you ever been to Gretna Green?" He kissed her neck, placed a hand on her waist.

She gasped. "Elope? Cassandra will be ruined, and we'll never be able to show our faces in society again."

He moved the hand to her breast, gently squeezed, wishing she weren't wearing a corset. "Would that trouble you?" he whispered against her neck.

She leaned into his touch, then groaned and pushed him away. "Stop, please."

He stopped, dropping his hands to his sides. Her expression was distant, definitely sad now.

"Yes, it would trouble me. I don't care a fig for society, but my mother does, and I do care about her. She'd be mortified, humiliated. And although I don't like Cassandra in the least, I shouldn't like to embarrass her in such a manner." Her expression softened. She cupped his cheek with her soft palm. "Lord help me, I am desperately in love with you, Peter Tenwick. But we must find another way."

His heart soared.

She loved him.

Armed with that knowledge, he would figure out something. He leaned forward until his forehead touched hers. "And I you. I will find a way, I promise."

He kissed her again, sealing the promise. They resumed their walk, hands clasped. The path did indeed begin to slant downhill, and it wasn't long before it opened into another room. The light from the opening in the wall was dim. They had been in the corridor for far longer than Peter realized, and the sun was on its way down.

"It's getting dark," Judith said, worry tinging her tone. "Perhaps we should go back to the house."

"You don't want to take a romantic stroll on the beach at sunset?"

"When you put it that way…" Judith tugged his hand toward the cave entrance.

The sky was streaked with yellow, orange, and pink, the sun a glowing gold ball hovering over the horizon. "Look how beautiful," Judith said, stopping suddenly, her eyes wide to take it all in.

"Yes," Peter said, watching Judith.

She smacked him lightly on the arm. "I meant the sunset, silly."

"That's beautiful, too."

They started walking down the beach, Peter making note of the landmarks so they could easily find the right cave again. The only sounds were the swoosh of their feet in the sand and the gentle lapping of the waves on the shore. It was possibly the most peaceful Peter had ever felt. For a moment, he forgot he had quite a few problems to solve before he could share his life with the woman who strolled quietly beside him, her hand in his.

"What's that?" Judith asked, pointing at a spot ahead on the beach. It was difficult to see in the dimming light, but it appeared to be a small boat. Men hovered around it, loading something onto a cart.

Before he could register the fact that there might smugglers on the beach, something cold and hard pressed against his back. He stopped and slowly turned.

"Bad night for a stroll, guv."

Judith gasped, gripping his arm. "Peter?"

The smuggler was short and stout, as round as he was tall, but the gun in his hand did not waver, aimed now at Peter's head.

"We won't tell anyone you're here," Judith said. Her voice was unusually small and quavering.

"We can't take the risk, can we, boys?" the man called. Three other men approached, pushing a wooden cart laden with large barrels.

"What have we here, then?" the tallest of the men asked. "Caught yourself some sightseers?"

The short man gestured with his gun. "What do you want to do with them, Tunno?"

The tall man, Tunno, whapped the short one on the side of the head with an open palm. "No names, idiot! We'll have to kill them now!"

Judith trembled, her fingernails digging into Peter's arm. Not willing to show just how terrified he was, he held his hands in front of him.

"Let's not be hasty. We won't tell a soul. We're not even supposed to be out here, or alone together. She'll be ruined socially were anyone to find out."

"Oh, no, ruined! We can't have that, can we?" Tunno said in a falsetto with an accompanying foppish prance.

The smugglers laughed heartily. Peter exchanged a glance with Judith, who now seemed less afraid and more irritated.

The tall man sobered. "Fine, we won't kill ya, but we can't have you running loose until we're well clear. Haven't seen the Waterguard yet, but they bound to be about somewhere."

"The Waterguard?" Judith asked.

"Revenue men," the short one said, waving his gun. "Fancy uniforms."

"Enough talk! They'll be passing by here in one of their cutters soon as it gets dark. Let's get this inside," Tunno said.

The short one prodded Peter in front of him, Judith at his side. He ought to do something, but he didn't know what. He sensed these men truly didn't intend to harm them. Though their purpose was serious, they weren't, particularly. The two youngest ones joked and laughed. They were strictly muscle, decidedly not employed for their intellectual prowess. They so resembled the tall man called Tunno, Peter suspected they were related.

"Boys! Stop messing about," Tunno said.

"Sorry, Pap," they chorused. The older man rolled his eyes.

"What are we going to do?" Judith's warm breath tickled Peter's ear.

"I don't think they'll hurt us," he whispered back. "We'll just have to wait for an opportunity to get away."

She nodded, expression resolute. She was no longer trembling, and if she was afraid, she didn't show it.

There was no way he was letting this woman go, whatever it took.

\*\*\*\*

Judith swallowed her fear. Peter's solid presence was comforting, and despite his unsuccessful attempts to convince the smugglers they were no threat she knew he would protect her, if it came to that.

But Judith hadn't grown up with brothers for nothing, and was certainly capable of saving herself, if need be. She studied each of the smugglers. The tall one, Tunno, was obviously the leader. The two boys, obviously his sons, were stronger than they were smart, and goofy besides. The short man with the gun at their backs was harder to read. He hadn't said much since their first encounter. She risked a glance over her shoulder, and his expression was hard. She didn't think Tunno would allow him to hurt them, but she knew he was capable of it.

At the entrance to the cave, Tunno directed the

boys to start unloading and scanned the horizon, presumably for the Waterguard. The short one kept his gun trained on them, saying nothing.

The casks unloaded, the boys covered them with tarps the same color as the stone walls. In the increasing dark, they were undetectable.

"Stash the cart, and let's go."

"What about these two?" Shorty pointed with his pistol.

Tunno put his hands on his hips and studied them for a moment. Peter opened his mouth to speak, but Tunno waved his hand. "I don't want to hear it, toff. Bring 'em with us," he said to Shorty.

"There ain't room for both of 'em," one of the boys said, then pointed at Peter. "Specially him. He's huge."

Tunno cocked his head. "Huh. You're right, boy, rare as that is."

He started to walk away, gestured behind his back. "Bring her, leave him."

"What do you mean, 'leave him'?" Judith's stomach clenched.

"This." In a surprisingly fast movement, Shorty reached up and slammed his pistol against Peter's head. The big man crumpled to the ground, a ribbon of blood trickling from his temple.

"No!" Judith screamed. Shorty grabbed her arm and began dragging her toward the boat. She fought against him, but he was far stronger than he looked. Peter remained unnaturally still upon the sand. "Peter!"

Shorty clapped a hand over her mouth and gripped her tighter with the other hand. "Shut it, or I'll do the same to you."

She tried to keep an eye on Peter, but it was full

dark now, and after a few minutes, she couldn't see him.

When they reached the boat, Shorty dumped her into it. She landed on her arse, her skirts tangled around her feet, her hair fully loose from its pins and covering her face. Before she could right herself, the boat was in the water and the two boys were rowing them away from shore.

Peter must be all right. She couldn't risk thinking otherwise. She couldn't live in a world in which he did not draw breath.

She simply couldn't.

## Chapter 13

"Oi! Wake up." Peter woke to the sound of a deep voice and a poke in the ribs.

"Stop! I'm not sleeping." He sat up, nearly swooned with the change in altitude. He closed his eyes for a moment until the world stopped spinning, then gingerly pressed the knot on his head. His finger came back sticky.

The day was breaking, the sun just beginning to peek above the water. He pressed his fingers to his forehead and his thumbs to his temples, hoping to ease the ache that started to pulse in his head.

The man who had roused him poked again with his boot. He wore the uniform of the Waterguard.

"Drunk, were you?" the man said. "Left here by your mates?"

Peter glared at him. "No, I was not drunk, and I was not left here by my *mates*."

The events of the evening flooded back into his brain. The cave, the kisses, the walk on the beach. The smugglers. And Judith.

Oh, God, Judith.

He tried to rise, but his knees buckled and he slid back to the sand. "I was knocked out. There were smugglers on the beach, and they took Judith. *My* Judith."

The guard sniffed. "There's no sign of smugglers

here, so I've only your word for it. You sound like a toff, but you don't look like one."

"Trust me, I'm a toff. I'm Viscount Caxton, heir to the Earl of Longley, and godson to Lady Howley, who lives up there." He pointed up toward his godmother's house, perched somewhere on the cliffs above.

"Lady Howley, eh? Not sure that helps you, lad." He sniffed again, spat a wad of tobacco on the beach at Peter's feet.

"What do you mean?" Realization dawned. "No. You think Lady Howley is a smuggler?" He leaned back, stared at the man openmouthed. "That is the most ridiculous notion I've ever heard. How dare you insult a lady of her rank."

The man shrugged. "We've had our eye on her for some time but haven't been able to prove it. Doesn't mean she's not a smuggler—she's just good." The guard put his hands on his hips and studied Peter for a moment, seemingly to judge his credibility.

Finally, he reached out to pull Peter to his feet. "Now what did you see? Could you identify any of the smugglers?"

"One was named Tunno, and he had two sons. There was another shorter man with them. They stored a number of barrels in the cave over there."

"We looked in there. Didn't see anything."

"They were against the wall. Under a tarp."

The guardsman spit into the sand, narrowly missing Peter's shoe. "Do you take me for a fool? There's nothing in that cave but sand."

Peter shook his head, setting off a series of shooting pains. He closed his eyes for a moment. "That's not possible. How long have I been out?"

"I can't tell you that unless you tell me when they hit you."

"It was after sunset."

The guard waved at the water. "It's sunrise now, obviously. You were out all night."

"They must have come back."

"No, they never do. Someone on the ground collected the goods."

"But that would mean…" He stopped. If his godmother *was* working with the smugglers, he had no wish to set the Waterguard after her. "No. I must have been mistaken. Maybe it was a different cave." He rubbed the back of his head. "They did hit me hard."

The guardsman narrowed his eyes. "Hmm. Come on then, toff. We'll get you back to Howley House."

"Wait—what about Miss Leslie?"

"Who?"

"The woman I told you about. Judith Leslie. She's been kidnapped."

"Are you sure you didn't imagine that as well?"

"Of course not!" Peter snapped. "We have to find her."

"Let's take you back to the house. Perhaps she's there, sound asleep in her bed. Perhaps she's in league with the smugglers as well."

"Don't be absurd. She's never even been to Kent before this."

"If she's not there, we'll send out a search party. The smugglers, assuming there were any…" Peter bristled, but the guard held up a finger to silence him, "…won't have gone far. They would wait for the morning tide to return to France."

"They can't have taken that little rowboat to

France. They must have met a ship offshore. They were Englishmen, from Sussex, perhaps, or Hampshire?"

"You didn't share that detail before." The guard frowned. "What did you say his name was?"

"Tunno. And he had two sons. Strong but rather stupid."

The guard nodded. "Very well. We'll be on the lookout for them. Now, come. Best get that head seen to."

\*\*\*\*

Judith huddled in the old fishing boat, pretending to cower but in reality studying her captors. Tunno, the obvious leader, sat in the rear of the boat and told everyone else what to do. Shorty was, as far as Judith could tell, a hired hand of some sort. It would not take much encouragement for him to turn violent, but so far he did seem to take his orders from Tunno. The two boys—Judith decided to call them Muscle and Bones—were obviously related to Tunno, most likely children. Clearly useful only for their strength. Even Bones, the skinny one, was strong—Judith had seen him lift the heavy casks in the cave with surprising ease. Muscle was older, heavier, more solid, with very little neck.

None of them paid her much mind once they'd cast off, but Bones did glance in her direction from time to time, a wistful expression on his face. She suspected he was the kindest, most vulnerable to suggestion, although what she might suggest she really couldn't say.

She wondered if they were planning to rendezvous with a larger ship and head farther out to sea—a situation Judith did not relish in the least—but the boat kept fairly close to shore and there were no other vessels in evidence, as far as she could see. Admittedly, given how dark it was, that wasn't terribly far.

Judith slept fitfully, fatigue overwhelming her despite an urge to keep one eye on the men. Her dreams were populated by a continuous loop of Peter crashing to the sand like a felled tree, blood gushing from a wound that grew larger with each viewing. She woke with a start after a particularly violent rendition, her stomach so tight she had to quash the urge to vomit.

The sky had lightened with streaks of pink and blue, and her captors were putting the boat into a small cove. It looked like any other small cove dotting the southeastern English coast, but she wondered if somehow they'd made it all the way to France.

Surely not. These men were English, through and through. But they had to get their goods from somewhere. What if they were planning to leave her here? Her heart slammed in her chest as she thought about what she'd do if they abandoned her here, wherever 'here' was. Or worse. Kill her here. How long would it be before someone found her? Assuming he was still alive—and she couldn't assume anything else—would Peter search for her?

The men had beached the boat and were pulling it ashore. Her stomach growled, allowing her to focus on something besides panic. She hadn't eaten for hours, and she was suddenly starving.

"Get 'er out of there. The boat is heavier with 'er in it," Tunno said, gesturing to the boys.

Muscle plodded over to her, nearly slipping in the sand, and plucked her out with one arm.

He lowered her to the ground but kept a firm hand on her shoulder, pushing her bottom into the sand.

"Where do you want 'er, Pa?"

"Tie her hands and stow 'er in the cave."

Muscle pulled a piece of rope out of the boat and loosely tied her hands.

"What do you plan to do with me?" Judith called out. Her voice was clearer, stronger, than she felt.

Tunno glared at her. "Why should I tell you that?"

Judith skimmed the desolate shore and let out a derisive snort. "Why not? What could I possibly do? Swim to safety?"

Tunno shrugged. "Fine. We'll stay here for a day or two, until we get the signal."

A day or two? God help her. "That doesn't answer my question."

"You'll stay here until I figure out what to do with you." His gaze trailed down her body then back up. Judith shuddered, expecting him to say something crude. He cocked his head and studied her for a moment, then surprised her by saying, "Wealthy, I'd warrant. Maybe we'll ask for a ransom."

"Ransom?"

He nodded. "Yeah. Ransom." He gestured to Muscle. "Take her inside."

Muscle hauled her to her feet and pushed her toward an opening in the cliffside. She had no idea where they were, wasn't even sure which direction they'd gone once they'd left the shore the night before, since it had been so dark.

The cliffs here were chalk-white, reaching so far toward the sky she could barely see the top of them. Inside, the cave had high ceilings and was brighter than she expected. Like the outside, the walls were white, glistening in the light from the torches Bones was lighting. Near the back, there were several pallets and bedrolls, and along another wall was a table and several chairs. A dozen crates were stacked nearby, along with a cask of wine. Bins held vegetables and fruits.

"Do you *live* here?" Judith asked.

Muscle shrugged. "It's dry and there's no rats. Better'n Portsmouth."

"Portsmouth? That's where you're from?"

"Shut up, boy!" Tunno barked from the cave entrance. "She doesn't need to know about us."

Muscle shrugged again and shoved her onto one of the pallets. "You can sleep there. I'll get you some water."

Judith hadn't realized how thirsty she was until the boy mentioned water. Now she tried to swallow, but there was no moisture in her mouth. She gratefully clasped the tin cup he offered her and drank deeply. Cold and slightly sweet, the water slid down her throat, easing the dryness. She wiped her mouth and held out the cup to Muscle. "Thank you."

He shrugged—the two sentences she'd gotten out of him appeared to be all he was capable of. He took the cup and joined his father, who'd dipped into the cask and poured himself and the rest of the men cups of what appeared to be wine. Bones took a bowl of something outside, and before long wisps of wood smoke curled through the cave entrance, followed by the smell of something savory.

Her stomach growled again, and she tried to remember when she last ate. Luncheon? How many days ago? It hadn't been more than twelve hours since she'd kissed Peter on the path leading down to the cave, even if it seemed like days. She wished he were here now. She didn't know how hard Shorty had hit him, but it had seemed a killing blow. She prayed he was unhurt.

Before her overactive brain could devise other dire scenarios, Bones came back into the cave with his bowl. He dished something into a smaller bowl and brought it to her. Smiling shyly, he held it out along with a hunk of bread. Grateful the rope around her hands was loose enough to allow her to hold it, she took the food and inhaled deeply. Fish, the salty sea.

"It's not much, miss, but I hope you like it." He moved some sand around with his toe. "It's salted cod I warmed in the fire."

"It smells delicious, Bo…" She stopped. She couldn't very well call him Bones to his face. "Please, what is your name?"

He turned to his father, who was busy berating Shorty. He whispered, "Henry, miss. My brother is George."

"Thank you, Henry." Now that she was so close to him, it was obvious he wasn't as old as she'd first thought. Sixteen, perhaps. "Would you join me?" she asked with a smile.

He shook his head and blushed to the roots of his hair. "Pa would never allow it. I'll get you some wine, though. P'rhaps it'll help you sleep. I, uh, noticed you didn't get much in the boat." He disappeared before she could say anything, coming back almost instantly with a goblet of dark, red liquid. "Here. It's French. Claret, I think."

Judith took a sip. It was surprisingly good, given the fact she was drinking it while a captive in a cave. "Mmm. It's lovely."

"I'll, uh, let you eat now, miss." Pink-cheeked, he

withdrew, returning to the seat at the table by his father, his gaze wandering over to her at regular intervals.

Judith took another sip of the wine. It tasted much like the wine Lady Howley had served at dinner. But perhaps one claret tasted like another. Or perhaps Judith was incapable of telling the difference. Either was preferable to imagining Lady Howley had purchased her claret from the smugglers. Or worse—was a smuggler herself.

She pushed the thought, and the wine, aside and finished her fish. Better for having eaten, Judith's head cleared. The men chatted quietly. She didn't know what time it was, had no idea where they were, or how far away they were from Folkestone. But surely it couldn't be that far—the boat hadn't been moving very fast, even if they had traveled all night. Time had seemed to stand still when she was in the boat, her heart aching and worried for Peter.

She wiggled her hands in the rope. It wasn't tied tightly, and her feet were loose. Perhaps, if everyone else fell asleep, she could sneak out.

As if he read her mind, Tunno barked, "Tie her feet, boy, so she can't escape while we get some sleep." He moved one of the pallets near the entrance so she couldn't sneak past him even if she did manage to walk.

Henry shuffled over with another length of rope, his feet dragging. He kept his head down, wouldn't meet her eyes; perhaps he felt guilty, or maybe he was just embarrassed to touch her ankles. When he was finished, he grabbed another pallet and laid down near his father and brother. Shorty snored loudly nearby, filling the cave with rhythmic, raspy whistling through his large nose.

Judith wiggled her feet, but they were tied too tightly for her to move them very far apart. Efforts to loosen them with her fingers were useless. She stopped before she made them bleed. Curling up on her pallet, she ignored the pain beneath her breastbone from her corset, thought of Peter, and willed the tears to stay away.

## Chapter 14

Peter and the guard arrived at Howley House an hour later, it being a longer journey up and over than through the tunnels under the house.

The butler answered his knock with a raised eyebrow but said nothing as he escorted Peter and the guardsman to the drawing room. Lady Grangemore, her eyes red from weeping, sat with Lady Howley on the settee. They both leapt to their feet when the men entered.

"Oh, thank the saints!" Lady Grangemore said, her gaze darting frantically around the room. "Where is my daughter? Is she hurt? Why were you out all night? Who is this man?" Lady Howley shushed her gently and pressed her back onto the settee.

The guardsman glanced at Peter, who nodded. "Stinson, m'lady, with the Waterguard. I found his lordship unconscious on the beach."

"Unconscious?" Lady Howley hurried to Peter's side, touching his forehead with the back of her hand. "My boy, are you quite well?"

Peter pushed her hand aside. He still had questions for his godmother and no time to waste if he were to find Judith. "I appreciate your concern, Aunt Gin, but I'm fine. I am far more worried about Judith—Miss Leslie, I mean."

"Where is she?" Lady Howley asked.

Peter tried to think of a way to break the news gently, but he couldn't. "She, uh, she's been kidnapped."

"What!" the ladies exclaimed together.

"Judith and I went for a walk on the beach yesterday, and we encountered a group of men I can only assume were smugglers."

Lady Howley's lips pinched together in a straight line, and the vein in her forehead began to pulse. She knew something, and she wasn't happy.

Peter threw her a questioning glance, which she ignored, and resumed his narrative. "They grabbed us, then took Judith and knocked me unconscious. When I was roused by Mr. Stinson this morning, Judith was gone."

Lady Grangemore had gone pale as a ghost, her lower lip trembling.

"I will find her, my lady, I swear to you," Peter promised. "I...care for her, more than you can possibly imagine."

Her eyes flashed. "You *care* for her? Then how could you let this happen?"

"I was only one man, my lady, against four, and I feared challenging them would only make it worse for us. I never thought they'd take Judith."

"You are too familiar, sir," Lady Grangemore growled.

Lady Howley patted her hand. "Now, now, Margaret, we are in no position to focus on social niceties at the moment. Besides, do you honestly believe Judith can go back on the marriage mart after this? When Lady Wilcox wakes up and gets wind of this, Judith's reputation will be sullied beyond repair."

What little color was left in Lady Grangemore's face drained completely. She moaned and fell back on the settee. Lady Howley exchanged a glance with Peter—one that promised to answer his questions—before rushing to the aid of yet another fainting guest.

Peter was entirely at a loss. Worry for Judith settled in his belly, a sharp, persistent ache. His godmother did speak the truth. Judith's reputation was in tatters, and he was sure word of this adventure was already winging its way back to London. It would be on the lips of every gossip in the *ton* by tomorrow morning, and there was no way his father wouldn't hear of it.

And when he did…oh, it didn't bear thinking on. Peter had to convince Kingsley to offer for Cassandra, and he had to marry Judith. As soon as possible.

But first he had to find her.

He turned to Stinson, who stood silently beside him, shifting his weight from foot to foot, acutely uncomfortable.

"I need to go after them. Where can I obtain a boat?"

Clearly relieved to resume discussing things within his comfort level, Stinson shook his head. "Do you even know what to do with a boat?"

"I live not far from the coast in Durham and have rowed on the Wear most of my life. Of course I know what to do with a boat."

Stinson gave a little cough but said nothing.

"You don't believe me, do you?"

"Rowing on a river is nothing like rowing on the Channel, m'lord, but I suspect I won't be able to stop you even if I try."

Peter shook his head. "No, you won't."

"Give me an hour then, and we'll set off. Best get a meal in you first."

Lady Howley diverted her attention from a groaning Lady Grangemore to address Peter and the guardsman. "Can I offer refreshment? To both of you?"

Stinson gave a slight bow. "I do appreciate the offer, m'lady, but I must report to my stationhouse and arrange for a boat for his lordship."

Lady Howley nodded then turned to her butler. "Please show our guest out."

Once the butler and the guardsman had gone, Lady Howley checked on Lady Grangemore, who appeared to have fallen into a fitful sleep. Lady Howley covered her with a blanket and settled her head more comfortably onto a pillow, then turned to Peter.

"I need to talk to you." She led Peter into the hall.

"I have some questions for you as well, Aunt Gin," Peter said, once she'd closed the door behind them.

"I expected as much."

"Did you know your caves were being used to store smuggled goods?"

She was silent for a moment, considering, Peter supposed, whether or not to lie. Finally, she looked him in the eye and said, "Yes. They work for me."

It was the answer he'd been expecting, but he was nonetheless shocked when it came. The next question came unbidden.

"Did you know we'd encounter them when you sent us to the cave?"

She drew in a sharp breath. "Of course not. How could you think that of me?"

"I just discovered you're a smuggler, Aunt Gin.

What I think of you has shifted somewhat."

"Fair enough." She sighed and fell into a chair along the wall. Her face was weary, showing her seventy-odd years for the first time. "I'm sorry, Peter. Truly. This is all my fault. I didn't expect the shipment until tomorrow, but I never should have left you to explore on your own."

Peter sat in the chair beside her, his large frame dwarfing the seat. "Why did you leave us? Of course, I know someone had to accompany Kingsley upstairs, but in retrospect, it would have made far more sense for me to do that. Leaving me alone with Judith would damage her reputation."

"Silly boy. That's why I did it. Then you'd be forced to marry her and would be far happier than you'd ever be married to the beastly shrew your father chose for you. Anyone can see that you and Judith adore each other. I was simply hoping to overcome your parents' objections by making it impossible for them to refuse you."

Peter's mouth dropped open. This was a side of his godmother he'd never seen. "You are a sly one, aren't you?"

"It's not as if you objected, Peter. You had to know what was happening, at least on some level. Or were you simply too eager to be alone with the comely Miss Leslie?"

"I will say it crossed my mind to object, but then…" But then he had glanced at Judith, whose lips were wet from her licking them, and all he could think about was kissing her.

"Ha! I thought as much." Lady Howley sobered. "But now we must rescue her from this fix I've gotten her into. I will leave a message at the pub and instruct them to return Judith unharmed, but it could be days before they get it."

"You contact them by leaving messages in a pub?"

"It's the way things are done here, Peter; the way they've been done for hundreds of years."

Peter shook his head. "I can't believe you're a smuggler."

Lady Howley shrugged, her shoulder blades visible beneath the fabric of her silk gown. "It was a necessity. And you'd be surprised to learn how many peers of the realm are involved in the trade. These big piles we live in are expensive to maintain, you know."

"If you were short on funds you could have asked Father. Surely he would have helped."

"Perhaps, but he has his own estates to run, and I didn't want to let on that Howley had left me in such dire straits. Besides, it's been an adventure." She patted his knee in a maternal gesture. "Now. I do have a boat, so you needn't wait for the guardsman to return, although it would be wiser for you to wait—he knows the coast far better than you do. I don't want to have to rescue you too."

"I'll be fine. I was perusing the map you have mounted in the library. How old is it?"

"Only about twenty years, but I have a newer one you can take with you if you're determined."

"I am."

Lady Howley nodded, her knees creaking as she rose from her chair. "Come, then, my dear. Let's rescue your lady."

****

The piercing cry of a gull woke Judith from

another dream-filled sleep. This time, fortunately, she dreamed of kissing Peter, not watching him fall, and was reluctant to let the images go.

She opened her eyes to see a beak startlingly close to her face. She jumped back, only to bang her head on the cave wall. She gingerly touched the spot, wincing as she willed the throbbing to stop.

The bird cried again.

Its eyes were yellow, its white feathered head damp. It picked at the sand around Judith's pallet and studied her boots as if they might contain a tasty morsel.

"Hello. What are you doing in here?" Judith asked it. She glanced around the cave, which was empty. Voices floated in from the entrance, as did the scent of something roasting in the fire. Her stomach growled, and the bird blinked.

"Yes, I'm hungry. I'll bet you are as well." She realized her hands and feet had been unbound while she slept—Henry, no doubt. She flexed her ankles, then rose and stretched her arms over her head, bending her back. She smoothed her skirts and her unruly hair and went out into the sunshine, the bird close at her heels.

"I see you've met Barney, miss," Henry called. He threw a piece of fish to the bird, who caught it midair and swallowed it with a happy squawk.

"Barney?"

"He's got a damaged wing, so he doesn't fly very well. Sticks close to the shore. He's a bit more like a dog than a bird nowadays, truth be told." He tossed another morsel.

"I thought I heard voices, but no one else is here. Where are they?"

"Pa and George walked up the coast a bit to see if the sloop is round the bend, just there." He pointed down the beach, where the rocks curved. "Shorty's off doing something. Morning ablutions, I suppose; I don't ask."

Judith didn't want to think about the man doing ablutions or anything else. "Is the sloop expected today?"

Henry shrugged. "We always check the appointed place and time, and if it's not there, we go back the next day." He shyly handed her a piece of fish, which she accepted gratefully.

She placed it in her mouth and chewed. Both sweet and salty, it was so tender it almost melted on her tongue. "What is this? It's divine."

Henry smiled, pleased. "It's lobster, miss."

"Truly? I've always had it drenched in butter, or in a stew. It's so delicate."

"That hides the flavor, but I bet you've never had it this fresh. Caught it this morning. They're not hard to catch—lobsters are stupid. I've got some traps over there," he said, pointing toward the water. Judith could see something bobbing in the gentle waves. "Then I just cook them inside their shells. You don't need to add anything to them at all."

"You should give up smuggling, Henry, and open a café," Judith said as she licked the juice off her fingers. "This is the most incredible thing I've ever eaten." She sat on the sand beside him, pleased when he offered her more.

They sat in companionable silence for a while, eating lobster and drinking what tasted like cider from ceramic bottles.

"Henry," Judith asked. "Will you let me go?"

He flushed slightly. "If it were me, miss, we wouldn't have taken you at all. Pa ain't a bad sort, and I know he won't hurt you. But we're expecting a big shipment, worth a lot of money. He didn't want you to interfere."

"Had you simply left me on the beach with his lordship, I think it would have been less interference than you'll experience now. And God help you all if he's badly hurt." She didn't want to contemplate worse—she'd never be able to bear it if they'd killed him. "They'll have the Waterguard searching for you, and you will hang."

"She's right," came a voice behind her, startling her so badly she dropped her cider. Shorty frowned at her as if this were entirely her fault. "Guardsmen are out searching the coastline—saw three boats coming this way. We need to take cover."

He grabbed her roughly by the arm and dragged her toward the cave before she could even contemplate yelling for help.

## Chapter 15

Peter eyed his godmother's skiff with some trepidation. "Are you sure it's seaworthy?" He walked around it, kicked the bottom. It seemed sturdy enough. Possibly.

"Of course it's seaworthy. Why would I send you out in a boat that wasn't? Your father would kill me."

"Somehow I doubt it. He's not terribly happy with me at the moment." When he had gone upstairs to wash, he found a letter from his father on his dressing table. 'Not terribly happy' was an understatement of monumental proportions, and the earl didn't even know about Judith's kidnapping yet. Phrases like 'shirking your duty' and 'disgrace to the family' appeared more than once. Peter shuddered to think what his father would do when informed Peter now *had* to throw over Cassandra and marry Judith.

"He'll forgive you, although I may need to give him a scolding first. It's not your fault you were put in a compromising position." Peter opened his mouth to object, but she held up a finger. "We've already had this conversation, and we'll say no more about it. I'm an old lady and can say whatever I like."

Peter laughed. "You've always said whatever you liked, no matter how old you were. Why should that be different now?"

"Exactly. Now help me push this." She set her

hands on the edge of the skiff and pushed. It slid easily toward the water.

"It doesn't appear you need my help, Aunt Gin," he said, but joined her nonetheless. Within a moment or two it bobbed in the waves.

"Get in; I'll hold it for you. There are oars, as well as some provisions." Once he had climbed in and sat on the sturdy wooden bench, she held out a map printed on oilskin. She pointed to a spot. "This is where we are. Head to here." She drew a line with her finger several miles to the west. "Tunno and his boys have a cave nearby, although I don't know exactly where it is. If I know Henry, he'll be grilling lobster, so you may see smoke before you see them."

"Henry?"

"The younger boy. He's not cut out for smuggling."

"I see. You really do know these men, don't you? Do you think they'll hurt her?"

"No, I don't, but Shorty is a volatile man. If he feels threatened…" She shook her head. "Let's not think that way. You will find them, and you'll rescue Miss Leslie. And your father may never speak to me again if he ever finds out."

"He won't hear of your role in this from me. But when he disinherits me, Judith and I will come to live with you." Peter said with a wink.

"Of course," she said seriously. He had been joking, but fear settled in his chest as he wondered if his father truly would cut him off.

"Now off with you, boy. Be careful. And Godspeed." She handed him the map and released the skiff.

He looked over his shoulder as he began to row away, but she was already gone.

\*\*\*\*

Judith chafed at the ropes which again bound her wrists and ankles. Shorty had stuffed a dirty cloth in her mouth so she wouldn't cry out as the Guardsmen approached. There had been a flurry of activity as the smugglers had smothered Henry's fire, used branches which had been stashed in the cave to erase their footprints, and then covered the cave entrance with a tarp painted to resemble the surrounding rocks. It wouldn't fool anyone who was walking on the beach, but it would be enough to prevent the guards from investigating if they saw it from the water.

All of them now huddled in the dark, as they couldn't risk lighting a torch. One of them had fallen asleep, as she could hear the snores—Judith's money was on George. She could barely see the outline of the two older men near the entrance, and the occasional glint of a knife in Shorty's hand.

What was he going to do? Stab the guardsmen? Panic lodged in Judith's belly as she attempted to imagine an outcome to this that didn't involve her dead body washing up on the shore.

She jumped when she felt a presence beside her. Henry.

"Are you all right, miss?" he whispered. "I wish I could remove your gag, but Pa would kill us both if you cried out."

Judith nodded, although it didn't do much to convey her thoughts, which were not suitable for polite company. Her mother would be appalled.

Which made her think about her mother, and the

fact she might never see her again. A tear leaked out of her eye and down her cheek, and because her hands were bound, she couldn't wipe it away. She pictured Peter. Kissing her. Winking at her. Lying pale and motionless in the sand. She growled from behind the gag.

"Quiet, girl," whispered Tunno.

She squirmed, trying to loosen her bonds, but they only grew tighter as she struggled.

"It won't be much longer," Henry whispered. "Please be quiet. I promise I'll untie you as soon as the guards leave."

Judith stilled. She wasn't going to get anywhere with her restraints. And she didn't want to cause trouble for Henry, however much she wanted his cohorts thrown in jail. He had been kind to her and had obviously been dragged into this life by his father. She felt rather sorry for him; in another family, he could have been a baker, maybe even a great chef in a noble house. Her mouth watered, imagining his culinary creations. She vowed if she ever got out of this mess she would help him break away from his kin.

Silence settled over the cave like an itchy blanket. Judith closed her eyes, tried to relax, to empty her mind. Anything to stop herself from dwelling on the fear and anxiety that filled her.

Finally, light flickered back into the cave, and she opened her eyes. Tunno had peeled back the tarp and stuck his head through the opening, then left the cave. Judith squirmed; her fingers tingled uncomfortably.

Tunno returned and pulled down the tarp, flooding the cave with sunlight. "They're gone, lads." He began to bark directions to the men, but Henry ignored him, focusing instead on freeing Judith. As the ropes loosened, pain poured into her fingers as the blood returned. She shook her hands and stretched her arms behind her back. Her mouth was so dry from the gag, she croaked as she thanked Henry.

Henry blushed to the tips of his hair again. He really was adorable, but he couldn't compete with Peter.

A shadow crossed over her, and she raised her head. Tunno was glaring at her. "Time to go, princess."

"Where?"

"Never you mind."

"Are you going to kill me?"

"Shorty would like me to."

If it weren't for the seriousness of their conversation, Judith would have laughed—it seemed she was not the only one who called Tunno's companion Shorty. She swallowed, almost afraid to hear the answer to her next question. "But you don't want to?"

Tunno spat in the dirt at her feet. "I may be a thief and a smuggler, but I ain't a murderer. And besides, you haven't given us as much trouble as I expected. By the time you get to civilization, we'll be long gone."

"Civilization? Does that mean you're planning to release me?"

Tunno ignored her. "Let's go." He grasped her arm roughly and pulled her to her feet. "Henry, load the boat with provisions. We'll leave anything we can't safely carry."

"Are we coming back here?"

"One day, mebbe. It's too hot now."

Henry nodded and grabbed a crate.

"Stop," Tunno growled. "What is that?"

"My cooking supplies."

"Too heavy."

"But, Pa, we'll need 'em."

"We ain't gotta cook, Henry. It's too heavy, and we'll have water to carry. Do you want to swamp the boat?"

Henry shook his head, his eyes heavy with sadness as he returned the crate to a spot along the wall. He grabbed a box of apples and slouched out of the cave.

"Your son is better than this life, you know," Judith said. "You should leave him here to make his own way."

Tunno's eyes widened. "I'll thank you not to be telling me how to raise my boys. Henry ain't no better than the rest of us."

"If you say so," Judith said, climbing into the boat before Shorty threw her in again. Planting the seed of doubt in the man's mind would have to suffice for now, as she couldn't risk angering him while he still held her fate in his rough hands.

****

Peter's arms, shoulders, and back throbbed with a persistent ache he hadn't felt since he rowed at Oxford. But he couldn't stop, not when Judith's safety was at risk. With every stroke of the oars, he had to believe he drew closer.

He hugged the shoreline, his gaze scanning the beaches and rocks for some sign of Judith. He honestly didn't know what he was looking for, but he would know it when he saw it.

## Chapter 16

After what seemed like hours huddled in the boat, heading God knew where, Judith couldn't help but wonder what they were going to do with her. Tunno had been clear he didn't want to kill her, but he hadn't been clear at all about what he *would* do. Leave her stranded somewhere? How would she find her way back to Howley House? She had left her reticule in her room when she had gone down to explore the caves, so was completely without funds. She would have to beg postage and write a letter to her mother.

But she was getting ahead of herself, assuming she'd be in a position to write anything. Tunno barked orders at Henry while George slept, oars held lax, his head tilted back and snoring. She was tempted to kick him but was afraid he'd retaliate, or worse, drop one of his oars so it would take even longer to get home.

Fortunately, Tunno did it for her, and George woke with a start, barely catching the oar before it slid into the water. She didn't quite smother a snort, and the boy sneered at her in response.

"Why don't we make her row?" he complained. "She's doing nothin' except eatin' our food and starin' at me."

"Quiet, boy," Tunno said before Judith could reply. "She's a girl. Can't be trusted to row us anywhere but into the rocks."

Judith couldn't let that pass. "I'll have you know I'm an excellent rower. Better than my brothers, at any rate."

Tunno squinted at her. "Is that so? Perhaps we should give you a try."

"I'd prefer it to watching *his* pathetic efforts," Judith said, glaring at George. Henry was giggling, so she grinned at him.

George threw his oars down and crawled to the back of the boat with Shorty. Judith took his place in the center and picked up the oars. For all her bravado, she hadn't had an oar in her hands in several years, her mother deeming the practice inappropriate for a young lady. They were heavier than she was used to and rough in her palms. But once she started, her muscles remembered. Soon she was matching Henry stroke for stroke, and they moved far faster than they had when George was rowing.

It felt so good to be doing something after what seemed like days tied up and in the dark. To be stretching her muscles, even if her arms strained at the tight sleeves and her corset pinched under her breasts. She hadn't given in, even when she was convinced these men would kill her.

She noticed Henry watching her from beneath his long lashes.

"You're good at this," he said, admiration tinging his tone. "Not even just for a girl. For men too." He blushed, dipped his head to avoid her regard.

"Thank you, Henry. That's possibly the best compliment I've ever received."

"Truly?" he asked, his head coming back up, his expression hopeful.

"Yes. Truly." She beamed at him as she continued to row. To take her mind off the blisters she was certain were beginning to form on her hands, she asked, "Where did you learn to cook?"

"My grandmother, mostly. Mum's mum. She liked to bake, especially, and didn't mind having me underfoot. I was sickly, so I had to stay home when my brother was out with Pa."

Apparently, it had been good for him. He was skinny, but strong, and seemed healthy enough.

"What's your favorite thing to bake?"

He cocked his head, his lips curving. "Apple tarts. Grandmother had a special recipe she got from her ma, who was French."

"What was so special?"

"Brandy. Apple brandy, called Calvados."

"Calvados. How intriguing. I'd like the recipe, if you can part with it."

"I'll have to tell it to you. I ca…" He paused, the tips of his ears turning pink.

"What?"

"I can't write."

Judith swallowed her pity—he wouldn't thank her for it. "I have a good memory."

He sighed, possibly in relief she hadn't said anything about his declaration. "Do you know how to make an apple tart? The usual way?"

"I do. Our cook makes a very nice tart, and she taught me."

"So do that, then mix brandy with sugar and some cinnamon in a pan, until it gets syrupy."

"And then?"

"Brush it on the tarts before you put them in the

oven, and then again when you take them out, when they're still warm."

"Mmm, delicious." Judith's mouth watered as she imagined the smell of apples and cinnamon wafting through the kitchen of her home in Derbyshire. "I'll have to make them for my family. Shall I call them 'Henry's Tarts'?"

He blushed again, his skin fairly glowing in the approaching twilight. "No, please don't. What if your family doesn't like 'em?"

"I can't imagine that."

"Oi, you two," Tunno said. "Shut yer mouths. There's something over there." Judith followed his finger, pointing toward a speck along the coast. Was it a boat? Perhaps the Waterguard was back.

"What'll we do, Pa?" George asked. "There's no place to put in."

"Maybe you should take your seat and put the fine lady back in her restraints where she belongs."

Just thinking of being tied up again made Judith's wrists chafe. "I'll be quiet, I promise. I won't say anything."

"Hmmph. So you say, missy. I'd rather not test your trustworthiness."

Shorty crawled toward her and took the oars away, shoving her toward the back of the boat.

"Stop it, Shorty." Henry shouted. "She's a lady. I'll thank you to treat her as one."

Shorty barked a sharp laugh. "Aren't you a hoity-toity gent, then? What will ye do to me?"

Taking advantage of the man's distraction, Judith grabbed one of the oars and swung it. The wood connected with Shorty's skull in a satisfying but rather sickening thud. His eyes rolled up into his head as his body vibrated, swaying dangerously until he toppled over with a splash.

"I'm sorry! I didn't intend to hit him so hard!" She raced to the side, looking for signs of life. "We have to stop."

Tunno shook his head. "We haven't time. That boat is drawing closer. If it's the guard, we need to put to shore. We certainly can't have a woman rowing."

"You can't have one tied up in the corner, either." Judith snapped. "He's your friend. You can't just let him drown. What is wrong with you?"

Tunno spat into the water as the boat drifted away from the site of Shorty's disappearance. "He's no friend to me. He's a business associate, and not a pleasant one at that. Chances are he'll come back up, spittin' mad and meaner than ever."

Secretly Judith suspected Tunno was right. Shorty seemed far too mean to die in anything other than a bloody gun battle. Nevertheless, she couldn't sit there and let the man drown. She bent over to remove her boots, but her stays made reaching her feet difficult.

"What are you doing?" Tunno barked. "You're not thinking of jumping in after him?"

"Of course I am, since you obviously won't." She managed to get one boot untied and tugged on it.

"Stop it, you damn fool woman. Why I didn't just knock you out like your gentleman and leave you on the beach I'll never know."

George snickered and his father turned on him. "Think it's funny, do you, lad? You jump in after him, then."

The boy paled. "Me?"

"You can swim better'n Henry. Get in there."

George tugged off his boots, then removed his suspenders and shirt, glaring daggers at Judith and grumbling under his breath. Judith barely registered the sight of his bare chest, far hairier than that of her brothers, before he slid into the water and swam over to the spot where Shorty had gone in. Judith kept her gaze fixed on the surface of the sea.

It was quiet, far too quiet, the only sound the lapping of the water against the boat and the creak of the oars against the wood. In the distance she could see the other vessel drawing nearer, but she still couldn't make out what it was.

Just then George's dark head burst through the water, sputtering as he dragged a motionless Shorty over to them. Judith and Henry helped to pull the unconscious man out of the water. Judith didn't miss the disdainful look George received from his father, as if he wished the boy had been unsuccessful.

Henry alternately pressed on Shorty's chest and forced air into his lungs, until the older man coughed up a great quantity of water. Henry rolled him onto his side, the water from his lungs pooling at the bottom of the boat.

Judith was relieved she wasn't a murderer, but she wasn't particularly happy to see Shorty back in the boat. It would have been far better for her had George taken him to shore. Tunno spat in disgust and turned back to the boat behind them, drawing ever closer. So much closer, in fact, she could tell it was a man in a skiff not unlike their own.

\*\*\*\*

Peter could see a small skiff ahead, nondescript

with chipped and fading paint, like any number of boats that dotted the English coast. But it was the only other boat here, and there were five people in it. It had to be the smugglers.

On it, someone swung an oar and knocked a man into the water. He slid underneath the waves and the boat moved away. Then there was obviously an argument. One of them was wearing a gown, but he couldn't tell from this distance whether it was Judith. Whoever it was, she was gesticulating like a crazy woman, and then a man half undressed and jumped in the water. Peter couldn't decide if he should row faster to get the woman away from them or turn around and get away from them himself.

The boat held fast while the man was underwater, and Peter was able to get closer. The swimmer resurfaced, pulling with him the man who'd fallen in. The woman leaned over the side with the rest of the boat's occupants and dragged the man in.

What the hell was going on? If this was Judith, why was she helping these people? Especially since she was the one who'd smacked him with the oar in the first place?

While they fussed over the fallen man, Peter drew closer still, and he was able to discern the color of the woman's hair—auburn, like Judith—and her dress, which was an olive green. There were four men, which was what Peter remembered of the smugglers. It was her, it had to be, and even as he was grateful he'd found her, obviously unharmed, he was deeply confused. She obviously wasn't tied up, and she certainly didn't seem to be in need of rescue.

Now that he was nearly upon them, he realized he

had no idea what he was going to do next. He had his godmother's pistol, but it was four against one.

Judith resumed her seat and returned her oars to the water. Peter began to have doubts—he couldn't imagine an earl's daughter could row so well. He'd never met a lady who could do so; his sisters would never even contemplate such a thing.

She was a strong rower, though. Her strokes were smooth and powerful, certainly stronger than the scrawny boy sitting in front of her. She reached up to brush something off her face, and Peter knew with certainty it was Judith. He had seen her make the same gesture a dozen times during their short acquaintance. His gut tightened as he imagined what she must have been through.

They must be forcing her to help, perhaps as punishment because she'd hit the other man and knocked him into the water. Was she being held at gunpoint? He leaned forward, as if another foot would make a difference in whether he could see more clearly in the approaching dusk. He shook his head, rowed faster.

But Judith was not only a better rower than her companion, her form was better than Peter's own. Her boat pulled ahead, lengthening the distance between them. If he didn't do something, he'd lose her.

"Damn it." He stood and yelled, "Judith! Stop!" His boat rocked dangerously, nearly toppling him overboard. He sat down hard, pain shooting up his spine from his tailbone to his still tender head. He grabbed his oars before they slid into the water and began to row again, faster this time. Pure need to catch her, to save her, fueled his every stroke, and he barely noticed the strain on his muscles.

His arms ached and his lungs burned, but he drew steadily closer.

"Judith!" he called again. This time he was rewarded with a hitch in her stroke. She turned in his direction. He could see her mouth move but could hear no words.

Unfortunately, Judith wasn't the only one who heard him call. The man who seemed to be in charge—Tunno, Peter remembered—pulled out his pistol and aimed it at Peter. A crack rent the air, and a shot plunged into the water ahead of the skiff.

"No!" Judith's voice carried across the water, and she lunged at Tunno. He smacked her as he would a fly, and she fell back.

Peter had never in his life felt so helpless. His heartbeat thrummed violently in his ears as the woman he loved tipped headfirst over the side of the boat and slid soundlessly beneath the waves.

## Chapter 17

Peter hesitated only a split second before removing his coat and boots and plunging into the water after her. It was cold, so cold it threatened to sap his energy, seep into his bones. But he barely felt it, so focused was he on finding Judith.

He quickly closed the gap between them, and dove deeper near the spot where she'd fallen in. The fishing boat had pulled away, leaving Peter to guess at exactly where she might be. The salt in the water stung his eyes, but he couldn't close them, or he'd be unable to see her. Time meant everything now. Lungs burning, his vision darted frantically through the blue-green water.

He spotted her dark red hair first, swaying in the currents above her head as she sank, weighed down by her sodden gown and heavy boots. He reached her in two great bursts, grabbed her arm, and pulled her close. He shot like an arrow toward the surface.

Above the waves, he sucked in great gulps of air. Judith was still, dead weight in his arms. She was pale, far too pale. He touched his lips to hers, tried to blow air into her lungs, but he needed to displace the water first. And to do that, he needed to get her back to his skiff. Shore was too far away.

He scanned the surface to see how far the boat had drifted only to find it coming toward him with someone in it.

The scrawny boy called out. "Give 'er to me, milord," he said, leaning over the side, arms outstretched. Too tired to consider any other options, he lifted Judith in his aching arms and handed her to the boy. He was stronger than he looked and easily pulled her aboard.

Peter used the last of his strength to haul himself into the skiff, landing in an undignified puddle in the bottom. The boy was tending to Judith, alternately pressing on her chest and breathing into her open mouth. Too out of breath to help, Peter could do no more than clasp her hand and pray, until finally, sea water cascaded out of her mouth and into Peter's already sodden lap. Peter turned her onto her side, stroking her cheek until she finished coughing, each cough followed by a sharp intake of breath, until she lay spent in the bottom of the skiff.

Peter pulled her into his lap, holding her close, comforted by the sound of her breathing smoothing out. Her eyelids fluttered and her bloodshot eyes focused on him. "Peter?"

"Shh. Don't talk, love. Just breathe. You're safe."

She struggled to sit up, leaned against him. He draped an arm around her shoulders, pressed a kiss to her sodden head. She gazed around, trying to catch her bearings. She stopped when she spotted the boy manning the oars. Peter had been so focused on Judith he'd almost forgotten the boy was there.

"Henry?" Judith said. "Where are we?"

"You're safe, miss. When you went over the side, I started to go after you, but then I saw this gentleman jump in. So I dove out of the boat and made my way to this here skiff. I thought you might need it."

"And you were correct, Henry. I am much obliged," Peter said.

"But where is your father? And the others?" Judith asked.

"Gone. Soon as Pa struck you, I knew I couldn't stay with him. I don't care what happens to me, but I couldn't let you die."

"Thank you, Henry," Judith said, reaching out to grab the boy's hand. "I will help you, I promise, to get you your bakery or café or whatever else you want."

"Oh, no, miss. I couldn't let you do that."

"Don't be silly. You helped to save my life. It's the least I can do." Judith shivered, and her teeth began to chatter. She leaned closer to Peter, but he was as wet as she, and no help at all.

"Henry," Peter said, pointing, "there's a stack of blankets over there. Could you hand me some of them, please? And take one for yourself. You must be freezing."

Henry obliged, and the three of them sat shivering while Henry rowed them to shore.

\*\*\*\*

Henry took them back to the mouth of the cave where the entire adventure began. Peter handed Judith out, then he and Henry hauled the skiff onto the beach, away from the waves. Every part of Judith's body hurt. It took all her remaining strength just to stay upright. Even through her chemise, her corset chafed against her wet skin, and her sodden skirts were so heavy she could barely walk. Her hair hung in soggy strands against her face, but she resisted the urge to push it away. Her hands were so numb with cold she'd probably poke herself in the eye.

Peter came up beside her and draped an arm about her shoulders just as Lady Howley emerged from the cave, Judith's mother hurrying close behind. Judith leaned against Peter, not a little afraid of what her mother might say.

"Judith! Oh, thank God you're safe." Lady Grangemore launched herself at Judith, pulling her into a tight embrace. "I've been so worried," she whispered. "I couldn't bear it if I'd lost you."

The sentiment was too much for Judith. She collapsed against her mother, and the tears flowed freely, soaking the back of her mother's gown. Once the shock wore off, she suspected her mother would not thank her for it, but for now, Judith relished the feelings of love and comfort flowing between them.

It did not, unfortunately, last long. Lady Grangemore pulled away and sniffed, dabbing at her eyes with the handkerchief she always kept stashed in her sleeve. She took a deep breath, then studied her daughter.

"You're such a fright, darling. At least you were wearing your oldest gown."

Peter pulled Judith tightly against him and dried her eyes with his own handkerchief. He turned to face Judith's mother.

"Lady Grangemore, Judith has had a very difficult few days. She needs dry clothing and rest." Peter threw a pointed look at his godmother, and Lady Howley led Judith's sputtering mother away.

"Thank you," Judith said as she watched her mother and Lady Howley disappear into the cave.

"For what?"

"All of it. For coming after me, for saving me, for sending my mother away. I was surprised at the hug, but I knew it wouldn't last, and I was right." She pulled her blanket more tightly around her shoulders.

"You're welcome," Peter said, tipping her chin toward him. He pulled her close and kissed her. His lips were soft, warm against her cold ones. She leaned in, disappointed when he finally pulled away. "I wasn't about to lose you to the watery depths, not when I could do something about it."

"You nearly killed yourself in the process." She shuddered to think of it. "If it hadn't been for Henry…" Her gaze flitted across the beach. "Where is Henry?"

"He ducked into the cave to wait until everyone was gone."

"We have to do something for him, Peter," Judith said, her tone insistent. "He only helped the smugglers because his father made him. He helped me. He gave me food, loosened my bonds. He was so kind and never once did anything to harm me. And he saved your life."

"Did I ever say I wouldn't help him? He saved you when I couldn't. For that I owe him everything." He pulled her close again, held her tight, resting his chin upon her head. Judith inhaled the salty sea scent of him, drew strength from his body.

"I do love you, Judith. I won't let anything, even my father, stand in the way of our being together."

"Not even your engagement to another?"

"No, not even that."

"You'll ruin her if you beg off."

"You'll be ruined if I don't." He traced her jawline with his finger, cupped her cheek with his palm.

"You're following in your father's footsteps." She

pulled back, immediately regretting the absence of his touch.

Peter shook his head emphatically. "I am not. He threw away the woman he loved for duty. I'm doing exactly the opposite. I don't care if he disinherits me, gives the earldom back to the Crown. All that matters is you." He placed his hands on her shoulders, kissed her again to emphasize the veracity of his words. It was hard for her to deny he loved her, impossible to pretend she didn't love him.

A throat cleared behind her, and she broke away from Peter. Lady Howley stood there, an amused, and if Judith was not mistaken, pleased expression on her face. She must have led Judith's mother back to the house then raced back.

"I trust your ordeal has left no lasting ill effects, Miss Leslie?"

Judith flushed. "No, my lady, although my head hurts and my lungs still burn a bit from nearly drowning. I am mostly tired of being wet. I think my garments are glued to my skin."

"Let's get you into the house. But first, perhaps we should see how poor Henry is faring."

Lady Howley was halfway to the cave before Judith realized what she'd said, and what it meant. "Wait. Lady Howley, how do you know he's there? Or that his name is Henry?"

Lady Howley turned and waited while Judith caught up to her. "I hired him, my dear. Or his father, to be more precise." She held Judith's hands in her own. "I am terribly sorry for what they did to you. Had I known they were on the beach when I showed you the caves, I would never have taken you down there."

Judith's mouth fell open. "You? You hired the smugglers?"

Lady Howley resumed her walk toward the cave, pulling Judith along with her. "I'm afraid I had little choice. Lord Howley left me with nothing but debts and this house; he had a gambling problem, you see." Judith was astonished at the matter-of-fact tone. She might have been inviting them in for tea. "It was either turn to smuggling or end up in the workhouse," Lady Howley continued. "On the whole, I prefer this life." She waved her hand, encompassing the beach, the caves, and presumably her sprawling house on the cliffs above them.

"Henry? Are you in here?" Lady Howley called out once they'd arrived in the cave. A figure emerged from the gloom within.

"Lady Howley," Henry said, offering a shallow bow. He nodded to Judith and to Peter, who'd remained at Judith's other side and now took her hand. His fingers were rough and warm.

"I assume you've left your father?"

"I have," Henry said, nodding. "He's a cruel man, milady. I'm tired of living under his thumb."

Lady Howley cocked her head and studied him for a moment. "You've no wish to turn him in, I trust?"

"Of course not. I'd only be punishing myself, and you."

"What are you going to do now?"

Judith answered for him. "I will make sure he's set up in his preferred trade. Wherever he'd like to go."

"You're too kind, Miss Judith," Henry said, blushing again to the roots of his hair.

"You saved my life, Henry. It's the least I can do."

Judith grinned at him. "But perhaps, Lady Howley, we could all retire to the house? I fear if I don't, I will smell of fish the rest of my life."

\*\*\*\*

After a bubbly bath that left her warm, deliciously fragrant, and rather sleepy, Judith ate a large supper alone in her room. Her mother had been given a sedative and sent to bed. Now she was safe and sound, Judith finally had time to think about the events of the past few days, and more specifically, all that had happened with Peter.

He was quite right—if they didn't marry, she would be ruined. She'd been alone with him for far longer than could ever be considered proper. She'd been kidnapped and held prisoner, alone with four men. She'd been half-drowned and rescued dripping wet by Peter and Henry.

She'd been kissed repeatedly by Peter on the beach. And elsewhere.

She sipped her claret and leaned back in her chair by the fire. Her toes were warm and her belly pleasantly full, but her heart was uneasy. If he didn't marry her, she was in terrible trouble. Not only would she be ostracized by society, she'd be miserable, for she couldn't conceive of a life without him. And Lady Cassandra, when she heard, would be more likely to dig in her heels and insist Peter go through with their wedding, just to spite Judith.

A rap at the window startled her from her musings. She set down her wine goblet and went to investigate. Peter stood on the ground beneath, his arm drawn back to throw another pebble. She unfastened the catch and raised the window, stuck her head out.

"What are you doing?"

"Getting your attention, obviously."

Judith settled her bottom on the sill. "You can't knock on the door like a normal person?"

"Well, no, then someone will have heard me."

"And you don't think anyone will notice if you break the glass with rocks? My mother's room is right next to mine, Peter."

"Which is precisely why I am out here, so I can run away if necessary."

Judith chuckled. "What do you want?"

"You, of course. I just wanted to see you one more time before you retire."

Judith felt warm all over. Was this what it was like to be loved?

"You are particularly lovely in your dressing gown," he said, a predatory glint in his eye.

With that statement, Judith realized it was highly improper he should be seeing her in her dressing gown. She removed herself from her perch and stuck her head out the window. "Goodnight, Peter. I will see you tomorrow."

"Do you love me?" he asked.

"Yes. Now go away before someone sees you."

"Are you sure?"

"Of what?"

"That you love me. For I love you. More than anything."

Her smile took over her face, from lips to cheeks to eyes; she imagined she was glowing. "Yes, Peter. I'm very sure."

"Good," he said. He blew her a kiss, then whistling a jaunty tune, disappeared into the garden. His tune carried on the wind, magical to her ears.

## Chapter 18

The next morning brought harsh reality. Lady Grangemore entered Judith's room without knocking, waking her from a sound sleep populated by dreams of a swarthy pirate with an uncanny resemblance to Peter Tenwick rescuing her at sea. She fully expected to find herself in his arms, and it was a rude awakening indeed to find herself alone in bed with her mother's half concerned, half angry visage hovering over her.

"It's time to leave, Judith," Lady Grangemore said, not waiting for Judith to wake fully. She stomped to the wardrobe and began to pull out Judith's gowns, tossing them on the bed. "This visit was such a terrible mistake. I can't begin to imagine how we'll repair the damage you've done to your reputation."

Judith sat up in bed, crossed her arms. "I'm going to marry Peter Tenwick, Mama."

Lady Grangemore pulled Judith's trunks from their hiding place behind the wardrobe into the center of the room. "No, you're not," she said. "He's engaged to marry another, and as charming as you are, you can't possibly compete with a duke's daughter."

"I've already won. He loves me, Mama, and I love him."

Her mother stopped fussing with Judith's clothes and placed one hand on her hip. "Love? Love has no place in marriage. I learned that from Lord Caxton's father."

"We cannot leave, Mama. I will not." Judith set aside her covers and rose, then proceeded to put her gowns back in the wardrobe.

"Stop it. What has gotten into you?"

"Mama, I was kidnapped. I was gone for two days. I nearly drowned, but Peter saved my life. I can't believe you're more concerned about my reputation than any of that."

Lady Grangemore dropped another gown on the bed and grabbed Judith into an embrace. "I was terrified—you took years off my life." She let go, placed her hands on Judith's shoulders. Tears shone in her eyes. "But you're back, you're safe, you..." Her face fell. "You are...intact, aren't you? None of those ruffians had his way with you?"

Judith's mouth dropped open. "You think...? No! No. I am fine, Mama. The smugglers didn't touch me."

Lady Grangemore sank into the chair by the fire. "Thank God." She took a deep breath. "Even so, there's no way we can keep this secret, not with the other people here. I'm certain Lady Wilcox has already written to half of London. Her fingers were stained with ink at dinner last night."

"So what are you proposing, Mama?"

"We'll have to go back to Derbyshire for the remainder of the season. Once Lord Caxton is safely married, the furor will die down, and by next season they will have forgotten it all."

A ball of acid gathered in her stomach as she thought of Peter marrying Cassandra. Surely he wouldn't marry her after all this. Would he?

\*\*\*\*

Peter went to breakfast with some trepidation. By now everyone in the house party would have heard what had happened. He suspected Judith would avoid everyone as long as she could, so he'd get no relief from that quarter. He paused at the dining room door, closed his eyes, and took a deep breath. When he finally entered the room, he was not surprised to find everyone except for Judith and her mother.

He nodded to the ladies, then went to the sideboard to fill a plate, ignoring the feverish whispering behind his back. When he turned back to the table, silence fell like a velvet curtain, and every one of the women wore a polite but vacuous smile.

He sat next to Kingsley, who was sitting as far away from the women as he could get while still remaining in the room. He grunted when Peter sat beside him but didn't speak until he had finished his kippers.

"Damn fine fish in this part of the country, I must say. D'you like kippers, Caxton?"

"Not particularly. I'm partial to bacon, myself."

"Nothing like a good slab of bacon, true." The duke took a sip of coffee and sat back in his chair. "So, I hear you and the lovely Miss Leslie had quite an adventure."

"Indeed we did."

"What do you plan to do now? She's quite ruined, I'm afraid."

"I plan to marry her, of course, although I've yet to determine how I will accomplish that."

"I don't see how Cassandra will give you up." He shook his head, gestured with his cup. "Dangerous business, old chap."

Peter leaned in to whisper, "As I mentioned the other day, it's not as if she wants to marry me anymore than I want to marry her. She's a duke's daughter, and I'm merely a viscount. Quite a step down for her."

"Perhaps, but you come with a deep purse, and Bothwell's desperately in need of one, or so I hear."

"Should Judith and I elope, do you think?"

Kingsley barked out a laugh, ignoring the looks it triggered from the ladies. "That's certainly one approach. It would ruin Cassandra, which isn't very nice. And your father would disinherit you."

Peter shrugged. "Possibly. I shouldn't like to harm Cassandra, but I don't particularly care if my father cuts me off."

The duke's eyebrows rose. "You don't care?"

"No, I don't. I should miss my sisters, the family estate, but how often does a man feel this way? I can't envision life without her, Reg." It was the first time he had ever addressed Kingsley by his Christian name, but he felt like a friend, almost.

The duke was silent for a moment. He ate another forkful of eggs, took a sip of coffee. "As I see it, then, you have three options. One," he unfurled one long finger, "you can go to Cassandra and ask her to break off the engagement." He held up two fingers. "Two, you can run off to Gretna Green with Miss Leslie, and risk being called out by either her or Cassandra's brothers."

"And the third option?"

The duke held up three fingers. "I have been thinking on this matter ever since we spoke the other day, when you mentioned she would throw you over if a better offer came along. It's rather perfect, actually.

I'll offer for her myself. I have more money than you do, *and* I'm a duke." He waved his hand in the air with a grand flourish.

Peter stifled a grin. His plan had worked beautifully, so beautifully, in fact, Kingsley thought it was his own idea.

But then he thought of Cassandra, and how mean she had been to Judith. How rude she had been to him. How generally unpleasant she was. Did he truly want to wish her on a man as pleasant as Kingsley? He opened his mouth to object, but the duke interrupted with a short laugh. "I know what you're thinking. I've known Cassandra for some time, and we are friends, of a sort. She is a prickly person, it's true, but she's also unhappy. But as my wife she'd have distance from her shrew of a mother and the freedom to do what she likes. Perhaps that would help."

Peter had a difficult time believing that.

"Don't worry, Tenwick. I'll suit her far better than you will. And it will save me from bother from these ridiculous creatures." Kingsley waved his hand again, this time at the mamas and daughters who strained, unsuccessfully, to hear their conversation.

"I…don't know what to say," Peter said, sitting back in his chair.

"Say you agree it's a brilliant plan, and I'll make my way back to London this morning."

"How are you…?"

"Going to approach her?" Kingsley asked. Peter nodded. "It's not as if I can suddenly profess my love for her, can I? No, I will simply be honest with her. I am amazed I haven't thought of this before. It really is an excellent idea. We are agreed, then?"

Peter nodded again, still a bit stunned at this turn of events, even though he had been the one to set it in motion in the first place. "Very well, we are agreed. But do you think *she'll* agree?"

"I can be persuasive." Kingsley winked. "I wish you every happiness, and I will expect to be invited to the wedding." He set his napkin on the table and rose.

"Reg," Peter said.

"Yes?"

"Thank you." Relief settled over Peter like a warm and cozy blanket, and the queasiness in his stomach abated for the first time in days.

"You're welcome." The duke nodded then made his way to the end of the table where Lady Howley was holding court and said his goodbyes.

Peter glanced down at his breakfast, now cold and unappetizing. He shoved his plate aside and stood. Assuming Kingsley was successful, Peter needed to propose to Judith properly. He nodded to his godmother, who nodded back, a little smile on her face. She excused herself from her guests, and he followed her out into the hall.

Lady Howley cocked her head. "What plan have you hatched with Kingsley?"

"It was entirely his idea. Well, mostly." Peter related the plan, and Lady Howley stroked her chin with one hand.

"It just might work. I'd always suspected Cassandra's petulance could be laid at her mother's door—when we are made miserable by one person, we are sometimes tempted to make everyone else miserable too. I think she and Reginald will be quite happy together. So now what you going to do?"

"I'm going to propose to Judith. But I need your help."

"Why?"

"Well, for one thing, I haven't a ring, and for another, I don't think Lady Grangemore will let Judith out of her sight. For all I know they've run back to Derbyshire in the middle of the night."

Lady Howley shook her head. "They're still here, although they are packing to leave. One of the footmen told me Margaret requested trays in their rooms. I can distract her long enough for you to propose, and I have just the ring for you."

She led him upstairs to her chamber. He'd never been in it, of course, and was a little uncomfortable. He'd known this woman for a very long time, but he'd never seen her private room. It was decorated in tones of pale blue, green, and gray, similar to the sea visible from the large windows. Her bed was a magnificent structure made from what appeared to be driftwood, the wood so weathered it was nearly white.

She noticed his regard, and said, "Howley made that. He was quite talented at carpentry. I always suspected he'd have been happier not to be born an earl so he could have spent his time carving things out of wood." Her expression was wistful, as if she would have been happier as a carpenter's wife too. "But never mind. I wanted to show you this."

She opened a drawer in her dressing table and pulled out a small, velvet covered box. She opened it to display a silver ring with the largest emerald he'd ever seen. The color was endless, flashing in the light of the morning sun streaming through the windows. It was a perfect match to Judith's eyes, fathomless and expressive.

"It's beautiful, Aunt Gin."

"It was a gift from my husband on our tenth anniversary. I'd like you to have it, to give to Judith."

He shook his head. "Oh, no, I couldn't. It must be worth a fortune."

She closed his fingers over the box and regarded him with a somber expression. "Peter, I will not live forever. I have no children of my own. It would give me tremendous pleasure to see this ring on your Judith's finger. Please, take it, with my blessing." She placed her other hand on top of the first and squeezed.

Peter kissed her weathered cheek. "Thank you."

"Now, go to the center of the labyrinth. I will send Judith to you."

## Chapter 19

Judith had wearied of trying to talk her mother out of departing for home today. Thoughts swirled around her brain, ideas raised then discarded, until she despaired of ever coming up with a plan. Now she sat in the window seat, the window open, gazing out at the maze in which she'd first encountered Peter Tenwick here in Kent.

As if by thinking she made it so, Peter appeared in the garden below, striding toward the entrance to the maze. His face tipped toward her window, his eyes lit up when he saw her. He blew a kiss and moved his hand in a "follow me" gesture. Judith nearly fell out of the window.

She chewed on her bottom lip, ran her suddenly sweaty palms down her skirts. She unfolded her long limbs from the seat and turned to her mother, determined to come up with an excuse for needing air, when there was a knock upon the door.

"Who could that be?" Lady Grangemore said in an impatient tone. She had nearly finished with Judith's packing and had only the jewelry to go.

Lady Howley entered. "You're not going, are you? What a shame! It's not because Judith is unwell, is it? Oh, there you are, Judith," she said, spotting Judith and throwing her a wink.

Judith's eyes grew large as she wondered what

their hostess was up to now. "I'm fine. Mama thinks it's best we go home."

"Do please stay for luncheon. Cook is making my favorite—cock-a-leekie."

Lady Grangemore stopped her hand wringing. "Cock-a-leekie? Truly?"

Lady Howley nodded, an enigmatic smile on her face.

It was her mother's favorite dish. Somehow Lady Howley was aware of this, although Judith doubted very much it was the woman's favorite.

"I haven't had it in years. My cook can't make it properly. Does yours use prunes?" Lady Grangemore asked, hope creeping into her tone.

"Of course. My cook is from Dundee, as you may know. It's divine."

There was no way Lady Grangemore was going to pass on her favorite soup. Judith nodded encouragingly when her mother glanced at her.

"Very well, we shall stay until after lunch. Judith, dear, why don't you go for a walk, if you feel up to it. We'll have rather a long drive ahead of us this afternoon."

"Oh, what a good idea, Mama," Judith said, trying to keep her excitement out of her voice. "I would so like to stretch my legs before we go."

Lady Grangemore narrowed her eyes. "Mind you stay in the garden. Don't even think of going down to the beach."

"Judith is a sensible girl, Margaret. Perhaps the maze, Judith? There are some lovely flowers at the center just now." Lady Howley winked at her, out of view of Judith's mother.

"Splendid. I'll put on my shawl." Judith grabbed the garment from the top of the trunk and slipped out before her mother could change her mind. She flew down the stairs and out into the garden, hoping she remembered how to get to the center of the labyrinth without getting lost. After a few turns, guided as if by providence, she arrived at the center, and there was Peter, reclining on the bench.

"It took you long enough," he said. She ran to him, nearly knocked him off the bench in rushing into his arms. Her lips met his, cold from sitting out in the wind. His arms reached around her, holding her close. She could not give him up, would not. She was resigned to eloping to Scotland, even if she never appeared in Society again.

His tongue delved into her mouth, and she moved closer to him, wanting to be as close as it was possible to be with several layers of clothing between them. She sat on his lap now, and she could feel his hardness through her skirts. Far from being afraid of what that meant, she was exhilarated, empowered by her femininity and her ability to rouse such a reaction from him. Judith Leslie, awkward and gawky, the ugly duckling, had captured the affections of this magnificent man.

Finally he pulled away, leaving them both breathless. "Not that I am objecting to such a greeting, but stop for a moment, darling. I have something to tell you." He set her beside him and grabbed her hand, holding it tight while he related his conversation with Lord Kingsley.

"Lord Kingsley is going to offer for Cassandra? Will she accept him, even if she's engaged to you?"

"He is a duke, and a wealthy one at that. Lady Cassandra said she'd release me from the engagement if I found her a suitable man of higher rank."

"She did? When? Why didn't you tell me?"

"Before I came to Kent. And I didn't tell you because I was afraid I wouldn't be able to find anyone. Marriageable dukes and marquesses are scarce at the best of times, and even more so this season. But then I planted the idea in Kingsley's mind, and it somehow took root, and here we are."

Judith kissed him, a reward for his cleverness. "Cassandra is nothing if not aware of social standing. When will we know what she has decided?"

"Kingsley has already left for London. He promises to write to me as soon as he has her decision."

"It will be a bit scandalous, Peter, rejecting you in favor of another suitor of a higher rank."

Peter kissed her again, and she allowed herself to be distracted. He broke away after a moment, ran his finger along her lower lip. She shivered.

"He is a very wealthy duke who needs an heir. She is the daughter of a duke who needs a rich husband. He is a much better choice than I, and she's already made it known that she's displeased with me. Tongues will wag for a day or two, but then the *ton* will move onto something else."

Judith prayed Lord Kingsley would succeed. The prospect of being a duchess would appeal to Cassandra, Judith knew—she probably thought of it as her due.

"And now, Judith, I have something I would like to discuss with you."

"Of course. What is it?" Judith expected him to talk about plans for going back to London. She did not expect him to kneel in front of her.

He was all seriousness, with none of the lighthearted joking she had come to expect from him. He swallowed hard, then grabbed her hand, kissed her knuckles, and held it to his heart.

"Judith Leslie. You are the most extraordinary woman I've ever known. You mesmerize me with your beauty, and you astonish me with your wit and intelligence. I cannot conceive of a life lived without you. I cannot promise we will be wealthy, or even that you will one day be a countess, because my father has threatened to disinherit me. I cannot promise we won't have to race to Gretna Green one step ahead of your brothers. But I can promise I will love you with all my heart until I breathe my last breath. Will you do me the incredible honor of becoming my wife?"

Judith could only stare for a moment, her hand warm against his chest, the rapid pulse of his heartbeat thrumming against her fingers. His face was all hope, love, passion. The rest of it didn't matter. Didn't matter where they lived. Didn't matter if they had titles or money. Didn't matter if they never saw their families again.

Nothing mattered but their love for each other.

Her grin was so wide she wasn't sure she could speak. "Yes! Yes, Peter Tenwick, I will marry you, even if we are poor, even if I am not a countess, and even if we must race my brothers to Gretna Green. I will love you with all my heart until I breathe my last breath." She pulled him to his feet and hugged him, kissed him until they were breathless once more.

"Wait, wait," Peter murmured against her mouth. "I have something for you."

"I already have everything I could ever want."

Peter reached in his waistcoat pocket and pulled out a tiny box. He opened it and held it out to her. A gorgeous emerald winked at her from within.

"Oh, Peter." Tears welled in her eyes. "It's beautiful."

"Not as beautiful as you are, but it'll do." He wiggled it out of the box and slipped it onto her finger. "A perfect fit."

She waggled her fingers, enjoying the sparkle of the jewel in the sunlight. Peter laughed. "You like it."

"I do," Judith said, grinning. But then uncertainty poked at her. "What am I going to tell my mother? She's still opposed to the match."

"We'll go to Scotland. You don't need her consent there."

"I know that, but I don't wish to." She pulled the ring off her finger, but he grabbed her hand, slid the ring back on.

"No. Your mother must understand this will happen regardless of her wishes. She must make her peace with this, or we will run away. It's as simple as that."

Judith swallowed. He had said it before but she needed to be sure he meant it. "You would give up everything? Everything, to be with me?"

"In an instant." Judith had never seen anyone so sincere. Love fairly radiated off him, enveloping her in it like a cocoon.

"Very well. We will tell her together." She rose and held out her hand to him. The emerald sparkled in the sunlight until he covered it with his fingers, brought her hand up to his lips and kissed it, letting it linger for a moment.

They left the maze, hand in hand.

****

"You what?" Lady Grangemore stared at the ring on Judith's hand, open-mouthed. Peter, Judith, Lady Grangemore, and Lady Howley were gathered in Lady Howley's morning room drinking tea. The other guests were blessedly absent, having taken a shopping excursion to Folkestone.

"I told you, Mama. I love him, and he loves me. We will be married, whether you approve or not."

"But he's engaged to another woman."

"I don't expect the lady to go through with it," Peter said cryptically.

"Why? What have you done?" Lady Grangemore narrowed her eyes.

"I haven't done anything. But I have it on good authority the lady may choose another husband."

"That makes no sense. Who?" She pinched her lips together and peered at him. "What's wrong with you?"

Peter shrugged.

"Mama, I don't want to go home," Judith said. "Can we not stay until Peter learns whether his engagement has been broken?"

"I don't understand any of this. Is he expecting her to cry off in a letter? Who does such a thing? I specifically told you not to pursue a relationship with this man, Judith. Why did you not listen?"

"Since time immemorial, children have been doing precisely the opposite of what their parents told them to do. I don't know why you're surprised, Margaret," Lady Howley said.

"Peter's father listened! Even when his heart told

him to do the opposite. Why should you get your happy ending when I did not?"

A shocked hush fell over the room. Judith stared at her mother, aghast at her outburst. It was only when she realized her mother was not looking at her but toward the door that Judith turned around. A man stood there, a man who greatly resembled Peter.

Lord Longley.

"Jonathan?" Lady Grangemore said, in a voice smaller and more timid than Judith had ever heard from her.

"Margaret." The Earl of Longley's voice was deep and husky, not unlike Peter's own.

"Father, what are you doing here?" Peter looked from one parent to the other and then at Judith, confusion etched upon his face.

The earl stepped into the room, eyes for no one but Lady Grangemore. "I didn't want to listen to my father, Margaret. I didn't." He crossed the room to her in a few large strides and clasped her hands in his own. "Could we talk elsewhere? There is much to say."

"We'll leave you," Lady Howley said. "Come, children." She stepped in between Judith and Peter and placing her hands on their backs propelled them out of the room and closed the door.

"What was that?" Peter asked.

"Apparently your father has come to a realization of some kind," Lady Howley said. "Best we leave them to it. But I think you may soon find that there will be no more objections to your union."

"This is your doing, isn't it?" Judith said, understanding dawning.

A tiny cat-in-the-cream smile graced the older

woman's face. "I may have written to Lord Longley and told him his presence would be appreciated by a certain lady of his acquaintance."

"So you lied." Peter winked.

She waved a hand in the air. "A slight untruth. At the time. I think it's becoming truer by the second." She winked. "Would you care for a turn about the gardens, my dears? It may or may not be possible to see into the morning room from one particular spot."

Judith took Peter's hand and they followed Lady Howley outside. For the first time since she'd seen Peter in his multicolored waistcoat, she was happy, truly happy. Certain, deep in her heart, that there would be no more obstacles.

It was, perhaps, naïve—she had felt this way before, and had been promptly kidnapped. But now the world seemed bright and full of possibility, and as she and her companions spied through the windows of the morning room from behind a tree, she knew her mother could feel it too. Lady Grangemore was wrapped in the earl's arms, being thoroughly kissed.

Lady Howley and Judith beamed at each other, but Peter turned away.

"What's wrong?" Judith asked, reaching for his arm. "Does it disturb you to see them happy?"

"No, of course not. I'm delighted. I haven't seen my father smile like that since, well, ever. But I've also never seen him kiss anyone, which is a little…uncomfortable." He stuck a finger between his cravat and his neck and rubbed.

Judith nudged him. "Oh, you baby. It's a beautiful thing. And you know what it means, don't you?"

Peter took her hands. "It means the last remaining

obstacle to our marriage is overcome, and you, my darling, will soon be stuck with me forever."

He pulled her close and took her mouth in a kiss that put their parents' efforts to shame.

## Chapter 20

The Earl of Longley made quite a splash at tea that afternoon, glued as he was to Lady Grangemore's side. Lord Kingsley's absence was noted and commented upon, at least until his mother quashed the gossip with a single withering glare.

Judith was sitting with Peter on the settee after another ear-bruising recital from Samantha and Rebecca, when Lady Kingsley appeared in front of them. She brought the tip of her cane down in a sharp thunk that nearly took out Judith's right foot.

"Caxton. I should like to speak with you." She glared at Judith. "In private."

"I have no secrets from Miss Leslie, Your Grace," Peter said. Judith could have kissed him.

"None?" The duchess cocked her head.

"None."

"Very well. Are you sure you wish to discuss this here?"

"That depends on what it is you'd like to discuss, Your Grace."

"Hmph. Upstart." She considered for a moment. "Take me into the labyrinth. I've seen you out there, both of you, so I know you are aware of the proper path."

Judith cheeks heated as the import of that statement hit her. "You've seen us out there?" she said, with a gulp.

The duchess waved her hand. "I've seen far worse in my time, Miss Leslie, don't you worry. Come, then, both of you, while it's still light."

The duchess took possession of Peter's arm, leaving Judith to trail behind as they went out into the late afternoon sunshine. The duchess had a very long stride for someone of her short stature; clearly her cane was used strictly for effect. Nevertheless, it wasn't long before Judith caught up to them and grabbed Peter's other elbow. He winked at her, warming her from the inside out.

They walked together, an unlikely trio, into the center of the labyrinth and Lady Kingsley sat on the bench, her neck at an odd angle as she squinted up at them.

"Sit, both of you. It's like staring into the crown of a tree. You'll have freakishly tall children."

Judith failed to hide a smirk behind her hand, but she did as asked and sat beside the duchess. Peter perched on the edge of a potted plant.

"I understand you've put Kingsley up to offering for the Bothwell chit," the duchess said, without ceremony.

Judith wondered whether she was annoyed or pleased by the development; from her neutral expression it was rather difficult to tell. She imagined, idly, that the duchess was a decent card player. Her expression gave away nothing. "It was entirely his idea, Your Grace," Peter said.

"Ha!" she barked. "I love my boy, but he's never had an original idea in his life. I will eat my hat if he thought of it without you planting it in his head."

Judith glanced at her hat, a rather sumptuous creation with fruit, feathers, and what appeared to be several twigs. Peter's thoughts were obviously along the same lines, for he said, "It would be a shame to destroy such magnificent millinery, Your Grace. I, uh, may have said something in passing."

"Ha! I knew it. Did you put him up to it, Miss Leslie?"

Judith shook her head rather more vigorously than she intended. "Don't look at me, Your Grace. I knew nothing about this until Lord Kingsley was on his way back to London."

"Hmpf," the duchess huffed again before returning her attention to Peter. "Explain, Caxton."

"It was actually Lady Cassandra's idea." He explained what she had asked him to do. "I simply told His Grace what she told me."

The duchess seemed mildly impressed, although whether it was with Cassandra, Peter, or Kingsley, Judith couldn't say. Then she began to laugh, a hearty bark not unlike the seals sunning themselves on the rocks at the base of the cliffs. Judith exchanged a curious glance with Peter.

"Good work, Caxton. I was beginning to despair Reginald would ever find a suitable match. She's a shrew, but she's undeniably pedigreed and will keep Reginald out of trouble." She smiled as her gaze snapped from Peter to Judith and back. "And Miss Leslie will make you far happier than Cassandra ever could. My blessings to you both."

She rose slowly, her bones creaking, and Peter rushed to assist her. "Thank you, but I'm fine," she said, waving him off. "I shall go back to the house and leave you two to enjoy the sunset. Sunsets should be experienced with someone you love, I've always thought."

Judith flashed Peter a quiet smile.

"You are certain of the way out, Your Grace?" Peter asked.

"I'm not doddering yet, Caxton." She accepted Peter's bow and Judith's curtsy as her due and left them alone.

Peter joined Judith on the bench. "What was that?"

"She seems pleased. It's not a bad thing to have a duchess on one's side."

"No, I suppose not." He took her hand, brought it to his lips. Judith started to lean toward him, then unexpectedly pulled away when something under the hedge caught her eye.

A magpie, its bright black and white feathers glinting in the last rays of the sun, poked at something in the dirt. Its long dark tail bobbed as it hopped around, tugging at something. "Peter, do you see that?" she said. "What is that bird doing?"

"It's probably after a worm, or something. What do magpies eat?"

"It doesn't look like a worm." Judith rose and walked over to the bird. It stared at her for a moment, challenging her, then emitted an angry squawk and flew away, alighting on a nearby branch.

Judith wiggled the object that had so interested the bird and pulled it out of the dirt. A glint of gold flashed in the sunlight.

"Peter, look! It's gold." She wiped off some of the dirt and held it out for inspection. "It's a ring, I think. It's terribly old."

"Perhaps Aunt Gin lost it. Is there anything else there?" Peter kneeled and brushed away the loosened soil. A bracelet revealed itself. He held it out to Judith.

Gold winked through a century of encrusted dirt.

The pirate queen.

"Peter! Do you think this is part of the treasure Lady Howley told us about?"

"I doubt it," he said with a disappointing lack of interest. He rose and wiped his hands with his handkerchief. "But we should tell Aunt Gin. Perhaps she'll recognize these."

Then he looked at her and laughed. Unlike the duchess, Judith was terrible at cards. She could never hide what she was thinking. "You think it's the treasure, don't you?"

She attempted a nonchalant shrug, but Peter clearly wasn't fooled.

"Come along, my little treasure hunter. Let's talk to Aunt Gin before dinner." He kissed her quickly, and they returned to the house, Judith clutching the two pieces in one hand and Peter's warm fingers in the other.

****

They found Lady Howley alone in her greenhouse, snipping orchids.

"I didn't know you had a greenhouse, my lady. It's lovely," Judith said. The sun had not quite made its descent into the sea, and the greenhouse, tucked into the end of the house closest to the cliff side, nearly glowed with the reds, yellows, and oranges in the sky.

"I enjoy it most this time of day. It almost seems as if one is outside, and when the sunset is as magnificent as this, it's my favorite room in the house."

"It is very nice, Aunt Gin," Peter said, a trifle dismissively. Despite what he told Judith, Peter did think their find might be part of the lost treasure, and he didn't want to talk about the greenhouse.

"Judith has made a discovery." He gestured to Judith, who held out the jewelry to his godmother. She cocked her head and studied them, then plucked a little brush off her worktable to remove a bit more dirt. The ring revealed more gold, as well as a ruby, glowing deep red even in the fading light.

Aunt Gin let out a long, slow breath, a faint whistle. "Where did you find these?"

"In the center of the labyrinth, at the base of a hedge. A magpie was trying to steal the ring. Are they yours?"

"They are not," Aunt Gin said, excitement creeping into her voice. "Do you know, children, I believe you've found part of Jocasta's hidden treasure."

Judith flashed him a gloat which was entirely adorable. He grabbed her hand and squeezed.

Lady Howley set the jewelry down and wiped her hands on her apron. "Come," she said, pocketing the jewels, and they followed her like obedient puppies through the darkening house to the library. It was a mark of her haste that his godmother didn't remove her gardening apron before leaving the greenhouse.

A thousand butterflies beat their wings in his stomach.

Lady Howley pulled a worn leather book off a shelf, then sat in the center of a long sofa. "Sit, sit," she said, rifling through the pages until she reached the page she sought. Judith grinned at Peter and they sat on either side of her.

"Jocasta was a meticulous recordkeeper," Lady Howley said. "She kept an inventory of all of the goods she plundered over the years; this book, supposedly, was found in a hidden drawer in her desk." Peter noticed Judith's gaze wander to the desk behind them. Lady Howley nodded. "Yes, that desk. Presumably she needed to keep this from her faithless lover as well."

She pointed to text written in a faded, spidery hand. Her fingertip moved down a list of items. "It's not clear how much of her inventory would have made it into her hidden stash, but if the ring and bracelet you found are listed here, we can be certain they belonged to her."

Peter scanned the list, his eye stopping at every mention of the word "ring." Finally, he spotted it. *Ring, gold with inset ruby. Maria Consuelo, Antigua, 1725.*

"Here. Look," he said, pointing. They continued to scour the list until they found an entry for a gold bracelet, from the wreck of the *Thomasina* off the coast of Barbados in 1715.

"So this is it. The treasure," Judith said. She wiggled a bit on the sofa, as if her excitement was a tangible thing, too violent to contain. Her expression had the same mixture of eager anticipation she'd worn when they'd explored the tunnels underneath the house.

"Possibly," his godmother said, reasonably. "We'll need to dig. Did you tell anyone else about this?"

Judith and Peter shook their heads. "We came straight to you," Peter said.

"Wonderful. Judith, I suppose your mother is no longer resistant to staying for another day or two?"

Judith nodded. "The last time I saw her, she and Lord Longley were giggling behind a potted palm in the drawing room. They're worse than we are, Peter."

Peter winced. It was one thing to fondle his own beloved, but thinking about his father doing the same thing was disconcerting, to say the least.

Aunt Gin smacked him on the arm. "Oh, you should see your face. One would think you'd swallowed a vat of castor oil. Allow your father his joy. We all deserve some." She rose and returned to the bookshelf.

"I'm happy for him, truly," Peter said, as it was true, then grimaced. "It will just take some getting used to."

Judith slipped her hand in his. "I think it's wonderful. You will too."

"Very well," Lady Howley said, and replaced the book on the shelf. "Now that's out of the way, I shall meet you here at dawn to start digging."

"Dawn?" Peter asked. He couldn't remember the last time he'd gotten up so early, by design.

"Yes. I'd like sufficient time to start before the rest of the house wakes up. I want to find and secure the treasure, if it's there, before anyone's the wiser." Aunt Gin rose. "Now, if you'll excuse me, it's time to dress for dinner."

She left the room, still wearing her apron.

Peter looked at Judith, then down at his dirt-streaked trousers. "I suppose we ought to do the same." He kissed her lightly, prolonging the contact until she broke away, breathless once again.

"That should last me a little while," Judith said. "I'll meet you behind the potted palm after dinner." She winked, then swept out the door in a swirl of yellow silk.

\*\*\*\*

Dressed again in her olive green muslin, a bit worse for wear, Judith snuck down the stairs at five o'clock in the morning, well before either her mother or her maid was stirring. At the bottom of the long oak staircase to the front hall Peter waited. Her heart gave a little leap when she saw him; she wondered if after years of marriage it would sit still, but somehow she didn't think so.

"I hope that dress brings you better luck today than the last time you wore it," he said, then greeted her properly with a kiss.

"Don't remind me, if you please," Judith said with a shiver. "I almost didn't wear it, but it seemed a good choice for digging buried treasure. Where is Lady Howley?"

"She's in the garden already, armed with a wheelbarrow and candles, in the event it's still too dark. You and I are carrying the shovels." He handed her a shovel she hadn't noticed he held, two more in his other hand.

They hurried outside. The sky was beginning to lighten, and birds sang their early morning songs. The grass was still wet with dew, making Judith grateful she'd thought to wear her boots once more.

Inside the labyrinth, Lady Howley grinned as they approached. "There you are. It occurred to me I didn't know exactly where you'd found the jewelry, so I didn't know where to place the candles."

Peter strode to the corner where Judith had challenged the magpie for the ring, although the bird was nowhere to be seen this morning. "Just here, Aunt Gin." He pushed his spade into the dirt.

"Careful, Peter," Judith said. "You don't want to

damage anything." Peter slowed down and Judith kneeled beside him, sifting through the dislodged soil with her hands. Lady Howley picked up a spade and started to dig nearby.

As they worked, the sun rose fully, casting shadows across the ground, warming the air. Although they had two good-sized holes, they hadn't found anything yet, save a metal toy soldier, three brass buttons, and several large rocks.

The magpie had returned. It perched on the edge of the large flower pot, its feathery head cocked, dark eyes alert. Judith tossed one of the buttons at him, but he ignored it. Clearly he was waiting for better.

Peter set down his spade and wiped his brow, leaving a streak of dirt over one eye. "We're getting nowhere. The staff is surely awake by now."

"I asked that they leave everyone undisturbed this morning and suggested they have a lie-in as well." Aunt Gin pulled a watch out of one of her ubiquitous pockets, consulted it. "We've got at least an hour before anyone stirs, I should think."

"Do you really think we'll find it here this morning, my lady?" Judith asked.

"I've grown used to disappointment. Over the years I've unsuccessfully searched every nook and cranny of the house and the caves, when the mood struck. It never occurred to me to search in the gardens. So while it would be exciting to find the treasure, I won't be surprised if we don't." She plunged her spade into another spot beneath the hedge and a metallic thunk echoed through the air.

Judith's eyes widened. "What was that?" She brushed the dirt away, revealing a wooden barrel with metal hoops, much like the ones she'd seen in the cave. Peter and Lady Howley both joined her in scraping at the dirt until they had uncovered the outline. It rested on its side, cracked in several places.

And spilling out of the cracks, a chain, encrusted with dirt.

A hushed silence fell over them. The bird had left its perch and stood quietly beside the hole, staring at the chain as if he too understood the significance of the moment.

"Thank you, Mr. Magpie. If it weren't for you, we might never have found this," Judith said. The bird cocked its head and Judith could swear it winked. It bobbed its head then flew away, as if its job was done.

"We did it, Judith," Peter said, exuberant. He plucked her off the ground and spun her around, something Judith had never experienced. Before she could enjoy the feeling, he pulled her close, taking her mouth in a kiss so exciting her toes tingled.

"Enough of that, you two," Lady Howley said.

Peter released Judith and returned her feet to the ground, a regretful expression on his handsome face.

"For the moment, at any rate." Lady Howley grinned. "Now, Peter, dear, I require your assistance to put the barrel in the wheelbarrow so we can get this inside."

"Where are you going to put it? You can hardly store it in your bedroom."

"It will go in the greenhouse. My staff is strictly forbidden from entering unless I have requested something. It is the perfect place to clean and examine the treasure."

Peter unearthed the barrel and tried to lift it, but he

struggled—it was too heavy, even for him. "Let me help," Judith said.

When Peter made no attempt to wave her away or say he didn't need a woman's help, she was rather pleased. Together, the two of them transferred the treasure to the wheelbarrow with minimal difficulty. Sometimes, her size was a distinct advantage.

"Thank you, my dears. Peter, I still need you to get this to the greenhouse; there is an outside entrance so we need not track through the house. Judith—I can call you Judith now, I trust, after all we've been through?"

"Of course."

"Then you must call me Aunt Gin, as Peter does. You should get yourself cleaned up. Your mother would have a fit if she saw you like this."

Judith's gown was stained with dirt and rust from the metal hoops on the barrel. She'd broken more than one nail scrabbling around in the dirt. "I think it's time to retire this gown, although I shall always remember the adventures I had while wearing it. This adventure, however, will be remembered more fondly than the other one."

Peter bestowed a kiss on her forehead. "Perhaps we should frame it."

"I think not. Go, darling, before Aunt Gin hurts herself trying to maneuver that wheelbarrow on her own."

Judith returned to the house, sneaking up the front steps and into the upstairs hallway toward her room. A door creaked from somewhere down the hall, so she darted behind a curtain at one of the floor-to-ceiling windows lining the hall. She peeked around the curtain to see who it was.

The Earl of Longley tiptoed from her mother's room, his cravat and coat hanging from his hands.

She was unable to stop a shocked gasp, and he turned in her direction. When he realized who it was, he grinned, looking so much like Peter that Judith almost gasped again.

"You've caught me, Miss Leslie."

She extricated herself from the curtain, then realized she ought to have stayed hidden—she had no good reason for being up this early, fully dressed and covered with dirt. "It appears you've caught me as well, my lord."

"So it seems." He paused, weighing her fate, then nodded. "Shall we say no more about it, then?"

"About what?" They exchanged an amused, co-conspirator sort of smile.

They started off in opposite directions, but Lord Longley called to her.

She turned. "Yes, my lord?"

"Welcome to the family, my dear. I'm sorry for trying to keep you and Peter apart. I hope you can forgive me."

"As it's obvious my mother has, I can hardly do otherwise. Thank you, my lord. I will make him happy, I promise."

"You already have." He smiled again and disappeared around the corner.

Judith hurried quietly to her own room, unable to stop herself from grinning like an idiot. It was fair to say this house party would be remembered for years to come.

## Chapter 21

*Four months later.*
Judith was nervous.

At long last, the day had arrived. She'd never thought her mother could be more difficult than she'd been at Judith's debut, but she was quite wrong. Lady Grangemore had insisted every moment of this day be perfect, from her gown to the flowers to the wedding breakfast. The entire *ton* had been invited, and when Judith peeked out the door at the assembled throng, she was certain every single member of society was in attendance, save perhaps for the King and Queen.

No one wanted to have to say they had missed it.

"Judith," Lady Grangemore snapped. "Do stop peeking. Someone will see you."

"Why should that matter?" Judith asked, closing the door.

"Because, my darling, your radiant beauty will draw attention away from the bride." Judith hadn't noticed Peter enter the room from the other door. He stood behind her, nibbled on her ear, neatly avoiding the emerald earbobs and pendant Aunt Gin had given her from the treasure. He twirled her around for a kiss, which even after three months of marriage still made her toes tingle. Since they'd wed, they couldn't seem to stop touching each other. They did try to limit their public displays, but in private...well, it was no surprise at all they were expecting their first child.

Judith's mother sniffed. "Good Lord. You two are insufferable. If you could pull yourself away from your husband, Judith, I would be obliged if you could help me with my hair."

Judith gave Peter one last kiss. "Shoo. Go see to the guests, please, and make sure my brother Andrew hasn't offended the bishop."

"Is he likely to?"

"You know him now, Peter. You tell me."

He shook his head, his expression amused. He stopped on his way to the door to peck his mother-in-law, and soon-to-be stepmother, on the cheek. "You look beautiful, my lady. You have brought a light to my father's eyes, and we are blessed to have you as part of our family."

Tears threatened to spill over, and Lady Grangemore sniffed again. "Oh, stop. You'll mar my paint." She poked at her rouged cheeks with her handkerchief, but her delighted smile reached her eyes.

Thirty years after they fell in love, the Viscountess of Grangemore was to wed the Earl of Longley. From their kiss in Lady Howley's morning room to this day, it had been a whirlwind. Lord Longley had apologized for his behavior, explained what had happened with Peter's mother. He'd told Judith's mother he'd only been able to bear his unhappy marriage by hoping she had been happy in hers. She had not disabused him of that notion, she told Judith, because it didn't seem quite fair.

After Lord Grangemore died, Lord Longley had been afraid to approach her, afraid she hadn't forgiven him, afraid he'd tarnish his children's memories of their mother, afraid he'd forever lost his one chance at love.

He was right, of course, but Lady Howley's letter telling him he'd been forgiven, despite its being a total fabrication, had stirred his fear into action. He'd realized he couldn't do to Peter what his own father had done to him, and it was worth the risk to ask if Margaret could still love him.

He did, and she did.

Judith tucked a few stray red hairs into her mother's elaborate coiffure, then fastened her hat on top.

"You are stunning, Mama," Judith said. "I'm so happy for you. So pleased you'll at last know happiness."

"Oh darling," her mother said, her eyes sparkling, "I *have* known happiness in the past thirty years. When you and your brothers were born, watching you grow, seeing them mature into the fine young men they are, and you turn from a gawky child into the beautiful woman you are today. All of that made me happy. Never doubt it." She kissed Judith, and they made their way to the back of the sanctuary.

The wedding proceeded as if in a blur. Words spoken, kisses exchanged, and a love that had endured enmity and loss was confirmed and committed.

At the magnificent ball which followed at Longley House, Peter danced with the new Duchess of Kingsley, while Judith danced with the duke.

"How are you getting on with your new bride, Your Grace?" Judith asked, glancing over her shoulder at Peter laughing with Cassandra as he twirled her about the ballroom.

"We suit each other," Kingsley said with a fond

look in his eyes, "rather better than I expected. She's far happier now, and kinder too. I hope you and she will be friends."

Judith wasn't quite ready to agree, but seeing Lady Kingsley enjoy her dance with Peter she thought it might be proof that Cassandra was not the horrible person Judith had thought her.

At the conclusion of the dance, Judith disappeared below stairs, where the pastry chef was putting the final touches on a beautiful cake, three tiers tall. Covered in bright white icing and violets, it was sure to be the talk of the *ton*.

"Henry, are you ready?"

"Yes, Miss Judith. Nearly done." Clad in a white coat and a chef's hat, Henry appeared happier than she'd ever seen him, even on the day she'd handed him the key to his very own pastry shop in Durham. "I think her ladyship will love this cake," he said, as he placed the last violet and stood back to observe it. "It's filled with chocolate—his lordship said to spare no expense. I don't know that anyone has ever made such a cake before."

Judith clapped her hands. "It's stunning, Henry. Everyone will love it, and what's better for you, they will talk about it. I'll fetch the footmen to help you carry it upstairs."

Hours later, satiated, satisfied, and deliriously happy, the newlyweds left for a holiday on the Amalfi Coast. Peter and Judith retired to their small townhouse, not far from Longley House in Berkeley Square.

After removing everything but her chemise, Judith pulled on an emerald green silk dressing gown and sank onto the sofa in their bedroom, removed her slippers, and put her feet into Peter's lap. As he'd done after every soiree since they'd wed, he warmed her feet with his large hands and proceeded to rub.

"Oh, yes," she moaned. "You have magic fingers."

"So you've said." He winked.

"At the moment, the only thing you're touching is my feet. But if you're very good, I'll let you work your way up."

"I'm counting on it."

His thumb dug into the arch of her foot, sliding up to the ball, back to the heel, massaging out the knots. The stress of getting her mother married melted away as her husband massaged and stroked. She was half asleep before she sat up so quickly she almost kicked Peter in the groin.

"Careful, darling, or that babe you're growing won't have any siblings."

"I'm sorry," she said, laughing. "I almost forgot something. I'll be right back." She kissed him and ran downstairs to the kitchen. She grabbed a plate covered with a cloth and hurried back to her husband.

He had poured each of them a glass of port and was sitting on the edge of the bed removing his cravat. She set the plate on the table.

"What is this?" he asked.

"It's one of your birthday presents."

"My birthday? I'd almost forgotten, with all the excitement." He started to lift the cloth. "May I?"

She curled beside him. "Please."

He lifted the cloth with a flourish to reveal a stack of flaky pastries. They were no longer warm, as she'd made them early that morning, and they smelled of fresh apples, cinnamon, and butter.

"What are these?"

"Apple tarts. Henry gave me the recipe, and Aunt Gin brought me the apple brandy when she arrived for the wedding. I'm quite sure she smuggled it from France."

"I thought she would quit the smuggling trade now that she has the treasure. She certainly doesn't need the money any longer."

"You believe that? She's addicted to the adventure, I suspect." Judith bit into a tart of her own. Sweet, tart, spicy; she'd gain a stone if she kept eating like this.

Peter kissed her. "Mmm." He licked his lips. "When did you make these?"

"This morning," she said, before taking her last bite.

"Is that where you wandered off to before dawn?"

"I didn't think you'd notice. You were dead to the world."

"I always notice when you're gone." He bit into his tart, and flecks of flaky pastry scattered all over his shirt. He moaned. "Oh, Judith. This is delicious. Promise you'll make them for every birthday."

Warmth spread over her. There was no pleasure quite like feeding someone a treat she'd made. "If you like," she said.

"I do." He popped the rest of the pastry in his mouth, then licked his fingers. He rubbed his hand up one of her bare legs. "Now, then. What was my other present?"

She climbed into his lap, straddled him. It was the only time she ever felt dainty. She ran one finger down the vee in his shirt, kissed his lips, his neck, his chest. "Perhaps another sort of sweet?"

"My favorite," he said, a moan escaping his lips as she pushed him backwards on the bed and her lips moved down his torso. "May I have this on every birthday too?"

She smiled up at him. "Until the end of time."

#### A word about the author…

Marin McGinnis is a writer of Victorian era romance who has spent almost half her life in a tree-lined, unabashedly liberal suburb of Cleveland, Ohio. She lives with her husband and son in a drafty, century-old house with their two standard poodles, Larry and Sneaky Pete.

When she's not writing, working in the day job, cooking for the family, or yelling at her excessively barky dogs, you can find her hanging out on her website at marinmcginnis.com, on Facebook at www.facebook.com/MarinMcG, on Twitter @MarinMcGinnis, or on Goodreads. She's a member of the Romance Writers of America and its Northeast Ohio Chapter.

http://marinmcginnis.com

Thank you for purchasing
this publication of The Wild Rose Press, Inc.
For other wonderful stories,
please visit our on-line bookstore at
www.thewildrosepress.com.

For questions or more information
contact us at
info@thewildrosepress.com.

The Wild Rose Press, Inc.
www.thewildrosepress.com

To visit with authors of
The Wild Rose Press, Inc.
join our yahoo loop at
http://groups.yahoo.com/group/thewildrosepress/